I0743101

Crimson Earth

A Collection of Short Stories on Ashura

Compiled by Nora Jamal

In the Name of God,
the Most Gracious, the Most Merciful

TABLE OF CONTENTS

Introduction

This project began at the close of August 2022 with an open call for art and writing on Ashura cosponsored by Harvard University's Project on Shi'ism and Global Affairs at the Weatherhead Center and the Ahlul-Bayt Collective. The prompt, The Brightest Light in the Darkest Night, featured a quote from Bibi Zainab who declared at the end of the day of Ashura that "I saw nothing but beauty!" Her words inspired a singular question in our hearts—what did she see?

Among the short stories below, some were directly written in response to this question, but in various forms and manifestations all of them engage with this gripping reaction to Karbala. The story of Imam Hussein in Karbala is one told every year across the globe and the tale of his tragedy living on in hearts more than a thousand years after his martyrdom. Mourning processions take place throughout the Middle East, South and South East Asia, and North and South America, where groups of Shi'a Muslims have lived in places like the Carribean for hundreds of years.

Many of our writers embody this diversity, hailing from countries like Tanzania and Malaysia, and each bring out the story of Imam Hussein in unique and diverse ways that all share the same message. These stories range from a depiction of the brotherhood of the sun and the moon, a conversation between Bibi Zainab and the Angel of Death, a reflection written by a 12-year-old Shi'a youth, and much more. Despite the multiplicity of perspectives and fictional approaches, all of the short stories before you aim to encapsulate the meaning behind the struggle of Imam Hussein, the Brightest Light in the Darkest Night.

After over two years of workshopping, designing, and bringing together these writings, we are honored to present Crimson Earth: A Collection of Short Stories on Ashura. May God bless you and this work, and may He hasten the reappearance of the Imam of Our Time.

The Cosmic Dance

Abdullah Al-Hurr

Abdullah Al-Hurr is a writer based in the United States of America.

For the inseparable brothers: Hussain, the sun that shall never set, and Abbas, the moon of the Hashemites.

Month after month, I am reminded
That my fate is tethered to Earth.
Spinning, I am, around it.

      Yet spinning, I am, around You.

The vision of Your light waxes and wanes over my face.
Trapped in this self-imposed cycle of sight and blindness
has left me with scars and estrangement.

I wonder,
      'Will this state ever end?'
I beg,
      Make me Your celestial companion,
And by You,
      I swear,
            I will spin in cosmic dance
            Until You break the bounds of orbit
                  And let me drift into Your eternal

flame.

The Sun and the Moon were brothers. The Moon wanted to be just like his older brother, the Sun. The Sun was not just the Moon's older brother, but a shining role model, leader, provider, protector, and guide.

وَٱلشَّمْسِ وَضُحَٰهَا

By the sun and its brightness
[Q 91:1]

The Moon revered his brother to the extent that he would refer to him by the honorific 'Master' rather than 'brother.' The brothers were as close as can be, and just as the planets revolved around the Sun, so too did the Moon revolve around his older brother.

وَٱلْقَمَرِ إِذَا تَلَٰهَا

...and the moon as it follows it...
[Q 91:2]

Until a day came where Allah's Will commanded that they separate. The day would belong to the Sun and the night to the Moon. It seemed to them that they would never be near each other again. They were to live out their days only seeing each other far from a distance. Allah—out of His Immeasurable Love and Mercy for the brothers—reminded them that although they would be separate, they were still within sight of each other and that the light He granted to the Sun, which was then shared with the Moon, was a manifestation of that Love and Mercy. The Almighty Lord reminded them that He was All-Hearing, All-Seeing, and always with them. He encouraged them to 'call upon [Him] and [He] will respond.'

Distraught by the separation, the Sun lamented the absence of his younger brother and missed keeping him warm amidst the deathly cold of space.

Similarly, the Moon cried at all hours out of fear of being alone, of which he was reminded by the absence of the warm embrace of his brother's light. The Moon's only comfort was that his older brother would shine so brightly that the moon would glow enough to reflect that light, and he knew that he was fulfilling the duty that Allah had commanded him to perform by illuminating the night sky with a dimmer light for mankind on Earth.

وَٱلنَّهَارِ إِذَا جَلَّىٰهَا

وَٱلَّيْلِ إِذَا يَغْشَىٰهَا

...and the day as it unveils it,

and the night as it conceals it.

[Q 91:3-4]

However, as each day passed, the Moon dreaded going on by himself. Had it not been for Allah, the Moon would have been completely alone in the darkness. Even the Sun would weep uncontrollably out of fear for his younger brother

being alone and far out of his sight, at times. The two brothers in their sorrow and loneliness prayed to Allah for help
in overcoming this trial. Allah, the Loving and the Merciful,
responded by conveying to them a prophecy wherein time,
life, and this material existence would eventually come to an
end—a moment when all of Allah's creations would return
to Him. Allah told them that at the end of time, they could
reunite in this material world before entering the next life.

وَٱلسَّمَآءِ وَمَا بَنَٰهَا
وَٱلْأَرْضِ وَمَا طَحَٰهَا
وَنَفْسٍ وَمَا سَوَّٰهَا

And by heaven and the One who built it,
and the earth and the One who spread it.
And by the soul and the One who fashioned it
[Q 91:5-7]

The brothers were comforted in knowing that they would
be near one another again. Day after day, week after week,
month after month, year after year, the Moon would revolve
around Earth and with the Sun shining on him, he would
smile and happily reflect that light onto Earth. As time
passed, the Moon only yearned for and loved his older
brother more because he knew of the Sun's greatness and
virtue, and that Allah had made him the source of light
for the whole galaxy—even the stars and asteroids would
whisper and roar of the Sun's merits. Using his brother as a

model, the Moon practiced improving himself for the day that the two of them would be finally reunited, so that he could present the best version of himself.

فَأَلْهَمَهَا فُجُورَهَا وَتَقْوَىٰهَا

then with the knowledge of right and wrong inspired it.
[Q 91:8]

Finally, the day came where Allah informed the brothers that they could be reunited. While the Sun had continuously embodied the Divine qualities and was Allah's most favored creation, the Moon had now refined himself to become the most perfect reflection of the Sun he could possibly be. Never before had the Moon's face shone as bright as it did now. And so, the pair had attained the satisfaction of Allah. After millennia of serving Allah and the Sun in order to help mankind, the Moon immediately broke from his orbit with the Earth and hurtled through space, rushing to his brother's side. Until, at last, he arrived.

The Moon passionately, yet humbly declared, "I've waited so long to return to you, oh my Master. I'm much older, stronger, and wiser than I once was. I have served you and Allah for millions of years. I reflected your light onto Earth as I was commanded. In every moment of my existence, I glorified you and Allah. As mankind looked up at me in the night sky, I proclaimed to them and the galaxy that I was nothing but a fraction of the light of my master, the Sun, who has been lit by the permission of The Light, Allah. As time passed each month, your light would shine less upon me until my face was untouched by it altogether and effaced by darkness. At that moment, I reminded myself and was reminded by mankind that I am no one. Mankind would look up to the sky and they would see nothing but darkness. I am nothing. You and your light, by the grace and mercy of Allah, have given me my purpose, my virtue, my face. Tell me, are you proud of me?"

After having listened to his brother lay bare the contents of his heart, the Sun, deep in silence, thought how best to respond, and then softly said, "The day you left my side was the day my back broke. And every day since, I have tried to direct as much of my light to you as Allah allowed me. I am the proudest brother. You honor me, but over these millions of years, it was your love for, obedience to, and hope in Allah that have brought you to the high and noble station of purity, morality, virtue, and merit that you now find your-self. And thus, they have made you good and deserving of light."

قَدْ أَفْلَحَ مَن زَكَّىٰهَا

وَقَدْ خَابَ مَن دَسَّىٰهَا

Successful is the one who purifies their soul,
and doomed is the one who corrupts it.
[Q 91:9-10]

In that instant, without having completed even a full orbit around the Sun, the Moon eagerly flung himself into his brother's solar flames. The Sun asked, "All your life, you have referred to me as 'Master.' Will you not call me 'brother,' just once? The Moon let out one last whisper: "I missed you, brother."

The Sun responded: "And I missed you, brother."

They reunited in the Presence of Allah and their love for each other, which could only ever originate from their love for Allah, magnified to such a degree that the Lord made it so they would never separate in the remaining seconds of this life and in the eternal next life.

يَٰٓأَيَّتُهَا ٱلنَّفْسُ ٱلْمُطْمَئِنَّةُ

ٱرْجِعِىٓ إِلَىٰ رَبِّكِ رَاضِيَةً مَّرْضِيَّةً

فَٱدْخُلِى فِى عِبَٰدِى وَٱدْخُلِى جَنَّتِى

Allah will say to the righteous, "O' tranquil soul!
Return to your Lord, well pleased with Him and well pleasing
to Him
So, join My servants,
and enter My paradise."
[Q 89:27-30]

Eternity in a Day

Nabeel H. Khimji

Nabeel H. Khimji is a writer, poet, and graduate student at Oxford University's Faculty of Theology and Religion.

Among the stars, the sight below was just as visceral. Angels created for the sole purpose of glorifying the Almighty were given leave to turn momentarily away from His throne and gaze upon the sands of Karbala.

I was finally given the command, as was the case billions of times before. But at this instance, I was met with teary eyes burning holes in my veil. They cried pools and yet every drop would boil and evaporate to steam on its way down, reduced to nothing before reaching Hussain. Millions of angels gathered around me as I prepared for my descent, limp-winged and shaky-voiced. My body was to carry out the deed but my mind wanted desperately to stay back, to weep and beat my chest with the rest of them.

In the vast expanses of the desert, Zaynab hurried back and forth, frantic to catch a glimpse of her dear brother, sensing the time was approaching when rivers of sacred scarlet blood would run through the bronze sand like the very veins from which they spilled. In those moments her body neglected its own thirst and tears began falling freely down her cheeks.

"Hussain! I'm with you!" The battle was deaf to her shrill cries, though her ears were force-fed the sounds of swords clanging against brass armor and men shouting battle cries, invoking the many glorious names of God as they disobeyed Him without remorse.

She stumbled upon a dune raised above the perpetual flatness of the desert, granting her hope that she might indulge in the sight of her beloved Hussain once more. She began ascending, her feet slipping backward as the sand ran beneath them. Even this short journey was accompanied by pain; her bones felt brittle and her muscles sore, reminding her once more of the children's hunger and thirst before her own. The view from the very top was as limitless as Karbala itself—she could see the tyranny on each of their faces, and the hypocrisy within each of their hearts. And resisting drowning in a sea ablaze with hatred and disbelief was Hussain, emitting the cool rays of divine mercy in every direction.

You must leave us, she thought, knowing what lay ahead, watching on as the mob took turns swinging swords and hurling spears at the ruby of the Prophet's household. The fateful moment was almost upon that holy land, and Zaynab felt a sharp pain in her heart, like a knife had been run across its walls, opening gaping wounds and stealing the blood away from her fingertips. Hussain took an arrow; it buried itself in his shoulder. He took another to the kidney, then to his abdomen, and another, and tens more after that until Zeinab could barely see her brother underneath the foliage of arrows by which he'd been pierced. And so began the purification of those sands as his fragrant blood trickled down from his wounds and onto the earth.

A weakness in her heart that only grew more relentless when Shimr kicked Hussain off his horse brought Zeinab to her knees, gasping for air, praying the chest upon which she saw Shimr climb was of a sacrificial lamb the likes of which saved Ishmael from beheading. But this wasn't the case, and Hussain was seconds away from being the very ram whose sacrifice would ensure the survival of his grandfather's religion.

In the moment Shimr raised his dagger over Hussain's head, all the dust from the furious battle settled. Every eye watching would know exactly what was to transpire, and the heart of every complicit body would bear the weight of betraying its Creator.

But as the dust's settling forced the tyrants into the moment, the clarity helped Zeinab see past what merely met the eye. I could no longer bear to spectate.
Down I descended, to Zeinab's dune, eager to serve.

"Salutations, dear Lady."

"And to you. I sensed your descent long before I saw your dusty, dark cloak and the black light emanating from your wings." Though time was frozen and the world around us was but a painting, still as the night, her eyes remained fixed on the scene ahead. "You're here for my brother," she sighed. And when I was afraid she'd weep, I wished only to bring her comfort.

"Say the word, my Lady, and an army of angels will descend from the Sun and reduce these tyrants to the very sand upon which they so pompously strut."

"It wouldn't be right."

"The Heavens, the Earth—existence is purely for the sake of your holy family. We exist only to serve you."

"I know, Azrael," she finally shifted her gaze away from Hussain and onto me. "But there is far more to the massacre than the bloodshed and the lives lost."

"What else, then?"

"I'll show you."

***

Suddenly the sands turned to fertile soils, and soldiers carrying swords were replaced by trees whose canopies met to keep the skies above from seeing what was taking place on the forest floor.

With his back turned to me and Zaynab stood a young man facing another.

They seemed rather alike; dark hair rested atop their crowns, their skin blended almost perfectly with the soil upon which they stood, and their frames were tall and broad and cloaked in the fur of other animals. Zaynab pointed to the one closer to us, whose face we could not see. He held a small boulder the size of his own fist behind his back. He trembled slightly and his entire body convulsed as though he was short of breath.

"It was here that I first met man," I whispered. Zaynab nodded.

Over the shoulder of his brother, Abel noticed her. The two locked gazes for a moment, mutually empathetic of the calamities that were to befall them that instant.

"What is it?" asked Cain impatiently, noticing Abel's attention wandering. He turned his head like a periscope, inspecting every inch of the foliage around them.

"What were you looking at?"

"Someone who's seen far more blood than you mean to shed today."

"What do you mean?"

"You're my brother, Cain. I'd never lay a hand on you."
As the chosen successor of the two declared this, the one entranced by evil's persuasive whispers inched closer. He

opened his mouth, inhaling shakily.

"I'm the elder," he finally uttered, his voice growing loud and impatient, his eyes fierier by the moment. Abel knew what was hidden behind Cain's back—and what he intended on doing with it—yet his eyes teared and glistened with a sort of disbelief that overcomes one only in the face of pure evil, the Satan who lives only in the imaginations of most for the majority of their lives, rarely making an appearance, suffocating onlookers as he's manifested in all his nightmarish grandeur.

Cain's mind was made up, overcome by the promises made to him by his own worst enemy.

The flapping of wings sounded all throughout the forest, growing closer and closer to the site of what was to be humanity's first murder.

Crows. They perched themselves on branches of the overhead trees. One began to squawk. And then another, and two more after that. Soon, an entire orchestra of crows became the forest's only ambiance.

"Please! Some silence," screamed Cain, pleading with the ominous birds who mocked him from every direction.

"Cain, I—"

"Shut up!" He kicked Abel to the floor, placing the boulder in his pocket and cupping both ears with his hands, searching desperately for a sound other than the squawking of crows. He heard nothing but the sound of blood rushing around his skull and the malevolent badgering of the devil.

Abel was still on his hands and knees, gasping for air. Cain wrangled him by his hair with one hand. With the other, he reached for the boulder and struck his brother at the temple so violently that the sound of his skull cracking in two split the deafening squawking of crows. Silence ran through the jungle as the prophetic blood from Abel's forehead ran through its soil. Though having witnessed it before, I trembled at the scene.

"Do you see the blood, Azrael? Coursing through the soil?" Zaynab whispered to me.

"I do," I managed shakily.

"A tributary of the Euphrates."

As we watched Cain retreat to the mountains, never to face his father again, I turned to Zaynab with sad eyes.

"Why have you shown me this, my Lady?"

"While evil returns an immaculate soul to its creator, it also burdens another with the grueling weight of an endless guilt. After Lucifer's rebellion against Adam, this was the second struggle between evil and righteousness, a struggle that my brother would inherit from his grandfathers."

The crows retreated back into the sky and we followed suit, soaring through the clouds painted golden as the Sun set on the fateful day. Night overcame the lands beneath us; I was uncertain how far we'd travelled.

***

We descended to the ground, into the darkness of a sleeping city. The earth beneath my feet was cool and a sharp contrast to the scorching sands of Karbala.

Whispers wafted through the still night's air. We followed them to a house, modest and built from mud. Through a window we saw a little fire sat at the center of a small congregation. They sat in a circle. Their faces, faintly flickering from the fire's jovial dance, pointed to one man. His eyes were a deep brown, housing large, jet-black pupils. He was thin, so thin it seemed he'd been fasting his entire life. The fragility of his bones was offset by the strength of his beard, which was as black as the night and so long it reached his chest. His was a soul I thought I'd never recall. Centuries passed before I was finally commanded to escort him back to the Creator.

He was teaching them something—something they weren't supposed to know. Their entranced gazes would be broken every so often by a paranoid glance over their shoulders. They were wary of being caught.

"I take it you recognize this man," Zeinab said before we heard faint cries in the distance. The small meeting of men in the mud house must have noticed them, too. They rose right away.

"What should we do?" blurted one out abruptly.

"They're going to have our heads for this, my master," said another to their bearded teacher.

The head of the group slowly raised a finger to his lips before tilting his head back, facing the sky, seeking Divine inspiration. He took a few deep breaths as the outraged cries from a distance grew louder and the men delivering them grew closer. Finally, he uttered, in an unusually relaxed, reassuring tone, "We will not be among the losers tonight. Our sacrifice will bring us victory."

"What could that mean?" I asked.

"The same thing it meant to Hussain," Zeinab replied. She turned to me. "The wheel turns for eternities before it finally breaks. And until the breaker arrives, each spoke spends its share of time at the bottom of the wheel."

"… Each apostle endures the hardships of the last," I added. Zeinab smiled.

Like clockwork, a mob of ferocious-looking men arrived at the scene of the meeting, confronting the congregation and its leader outside the mud house. Looking on, I noticed a stark difference between the two parties. On one side stood a rather modest bunch, sporting unkempt hair and tattered rags, though their faces beamed with a light resembling that of generations of noble companions; Salman and Jabir, Habib and Abbas. On the other side stood a much larger crew of men sporting silk garments and ornate jewelry— even in the middle of the night. These uppity men were clearly both the originators and the enforcers of the law of that land.

"It's Noah once more!" shouted the leader of the group adorned in gold and fine fabrics. He led the pack. His cronies laughed a cruel, demeaning laugh. They all bore a strong resemblance to Cain.

Noah stepped forward. His build wasn't muscular like that of his opposition. But the straightness with which he stood—the uprightness of prophethood—made him tower over them by miles. His head was in the clouds and no matter how far back they tilted theirs, the sons of Cain just couldn't meet their eyes with his.

"It's the dead of night," said the tyrant.

"That it is," replied Noah.

"And the city sleeps."

"That it does."

"With the exception of you and these… Street-dwellers."

"By God, the holes in their robes are more blessed than you and your households."

The tyrant wore an expression of shock. He raised his eyebrows and stuck his neck forward slightly, as though he was waiting for Noah to revise his statement.

"Pardon me, O deranged, old man, but while our households prosper off the bounties of the earth, yours eat leaves and serve our families at our whim. You are all leagues beneath us, and your midnight gatherings are forbidden!"

Noah was unfazed, almost disinterested. "Be that as it may," he responded calmly, "we're not answerable to you, but to a power far greater."

"Your insanity has plagued our city for far too long!"

"You say insanity runs through me, but blindness afflicts all of you."

"Enough!" shouted the tyrant. A bead of sweat ran down his temple and over a vein pulsing violently under his skin. His jaw was clenched tightly—any tighter and his bottom row of teeth might've ground the top row to dust. He turned around, facing his men, who'd been positioned to pounce since the very beginning of the skirmish, like tigers stalking prey. "Show them discipline and leave not a single one untouched."

To call it a massacre would be an understatement. The clothes on Noah and his men matched the rubies worn by their attackers. At the close of the ambush, in the midst of scattered, lifeless bodies, Zeinab searched for the messenger's. He wasn't hard to spot. She followed his fragrance, a heavenly scent.

"Like my grandfather's," she said, following its trail. "Like Hussain's."

She knelt beside Noah's body, bruises on his arms and blood seeping from his ears.

"Here we are, Azrael, where good and evil collide and the wicked take lives at the expense of their own souls."

The ark rocked gently from side to side, in harmony with the water upon which it floated, a motion so calming to the nerves I didn't question where the past hundreds of years had gone. It was like a palace on the sea, and we stood at the deck's railing, marveling at its aquatic dominion. Beside us approached Noah, of the same thin stature, but limbs that trembled as he moved them; turning an infinite number of date palms to a castle-sized ark strong enough to bear the force of an apocalyptic flood had taxed him physically. His long beard, now a silvery grey, glittered, reflecting the small bursts of sunlight that bounced off every single ripple in the water around the ark.

We silently observed Divine majesty in the form of an ocean that had fallen from the sky.

"God is great," sighed Noah, the corners of his lips turning up.

"Azrael," he shifted, "aren't you a bit early for our meeting?"

"Today I'm a mere traveling companion, Prophet of God," I replied, delighted by his address.

"Praise be to Him," added Zeinab. "How long has it been," she inquired, "since the night of the ambush?"

"A millennium, give or take."

"Aren't you tired?"

"On this ark I host the entirety of our Lord's creation. I bore the responsibility of guiding mankind on the righteous path for hundreds of years. And at the very onset of this voyage, my own son, Canaan, and my wife, Rabi'a, rejected the truth and drowned in their own arrogance. I could not have persevered through all this had I been operating on the energy of an ordinary man."

"Sorry," I interjected, "but how does one escape being an 'ordinary man'?"

"If one lives as a man of faith, millennia of hardships flash in an instant. The
moments we truly absorb and remember are ones like these, where we stand awestruck by the power of the Divine."

"Is that why we're here?" I questioned further. "Why we witnessed the death of Abel? Your victory over the disbelievers?"

"You witnessed neither the death of Abel nor a victory attributable to me."
Curious.

"What, then?"

"What you've seen are collisions between the righteous and the false," continued Noah, "where the latter is either extinguished by the former or consumed by itself."

"Azrael," Zaynab began. "The world is a stage upon which this conflict becomes manifest millions of times. As the distance between man and God grows, toil and sacrifice pave his path back to the Origin."

"I see," I replied, trailing off as we continued gazing into the crystal-clear water. In it, however, I saw not our reflections, but a tree stump a few feet wide sat in a luscious, green meadow. And before I could look over at Noah and ask him if he saw the same, we were there.

***

As we made our descent we encountered Gabriel, who was on his way back up to the Heavens. Zeinab and I saluted him before landing.

We saw an old man at the stump. His back was turned to us and on the stump lay the carcass of a ram. Each strike of his cleaver detached yet another limb. The air was still and the only sounds bouncing through it were those of metal slicing through flesh and being wedged into wood. Nearby the makeshift butcher's board was a whole tree at whose base lounged a young man with dark hair and fair skin. He was eating an apple; each bite drew me to the raw cuts and bruises on his wrists, as though he'd been bound.

Our footsteps grew closer, louder. The old man paused his cleaving, his curly, grey hair, which once bounced with each swift slice, stood still. He rose slowly and turned to greet us.

The young man at the tree did the same.

"Salutations, Grandfather," uttered Zeinab gently, maintaining the meadow's peace.

"And to you, Zeinab," he replied with kind eyes. "And you as well, Azrael."

"Peace be upon you, O prophets of God," I replied, addressing the man and his son.

"Ishmael," he turned, calling out to the young man. "Come greet your granddaughter." He joined his father and greeted us both. "How fitting," Abraham continued, "that my sacrifice and Hussain's occur on the same day." Zeinab smiled.

"Fitting, indeed," she began. "But all sacrifices are one, carried out simultaneously, in the end." This perplexed me.

"How could that be?" I asked. "We're centuries in the past… Hussain isn't in Kerbala right now."

"Then why is it," Abraham replied thoughtfully, "that the only reason I've butchered a ram instead of my son, Ishmael, is that Hussain offered his own children on the day of Ashura?" I was jarred. I looked at Abraham, then at Zeinab.

"We have more to see," she said.

***

The palace was dark, lit only by a few torches lining the grand marble pillars flanking the throne room's central pathway. The walk from the entrance to the elevated platform upon which the King received his subjects was long. The King aside, his attendants were a greater indication of the city's departure from goodness. Their faces housed scowls and their hands were glued to their swords' pommels, ready to unsheathe at the clap of a hand.

The King himself was pompous. His spine made no contact with the back of his great chair; he sat upright with his chin held high. When subjects sought an audience with him, they'd meet his nostrils sooner than his eyes.

As we approached the palace's bounds, before entering its premises, we heard whispers that the King was once good, and that his sister and her daughter, his niece, changed his allegiance. Zaynab confirmed the rumors.

"He fell in love with her," she told me as we approached the gates. "As soon as her mother learned of it, she pushed her not to loosen her grip on her uncle until she was made queen."

On that day, before the King and his young bride, who were themselves cloaked in silk and adorned in jewels, stood a modest outsider. His mission was simple. He wished for them to return to the path of the righteous.

"Who sent you?" questioned the King. His crown almost slid off his head due to the tilt of his neck. His eyes glimmered with curiosity.

"My cousin. A man by the name of Jesus," the man began, "wished for me to convince you out of your unholy commitment."

"I've heard of your cousin," replied the King. "Which means you must be John, the Baptist." John nodded. The King's rage simmered for a moment, then boiled over. "My people have lived by a certain code for generations and I don't intend on reversing that code at the whim of some foreign heretic!"

"God wishes you to be a guardian over this woman, good King," John responded, "not her husband!" Until that point the King's niece was silent. But her own rage had bubbled away for long enough and it finally exploded forth.

"Silence!" she demanded, her shrill cry echoing throughout the great hall. "Your teachings carry no weight here. I command you to have this false prophet executed!" The King began to protest, claiming her orders were too severe. But she insisted. "Nothing must come between a King and his beloved. Today, he'll dictate our marriages, tomorrow he'll steal the kingdom altogether." Suddenly he was convinced.

We rushed to John, who was forced onto his knees and bound with rope for the execution.

"Peace be upon you, Zeinab," he smiled. "And you, Azrael," he continued, "you're on time."

"And on you, O faithful apostle of God," Zeinab replied.

"My prophet," I began, "I regret seeing you in this state once more."

"Now that we meet here a second time," John replied, "you should know that my father, Zechariah, pled with God to grant him a son he would love dearly, and with whom he would be tormented the way Muhammad, Ali, and Fatima are tormented through Hussain."

"I want his head!" demanded the queen-to-be before a servant emerged from behind the throne delicately carrying a golden platter. The air was stiff, silent. The only sound past that point was that of a sword jumping out of its sheath.

"Azrael," John whispered to me. I looked into his eyes a final time. "It isn't my head bound for that tray."

Upon those words, the palace's cold walls became Karbala's relentless Sun. The scene was the same; Shimr still sat atop the chest of Hussain. And yet, everything appeared different.

***

"You see it now, don't you, Azrael?"

"Muhammad's predecessors, each and every single one of them, knew of Hussain's sacrifice. They praised him."

"Yes," Zaynab replied, gazing out at the battlefield. "Hussain was alive during their times, from the very beginning, and he will remain so after today."

"Then why must Karbala be a slaughterhouse?"

"So that people might see their entire pasts and futures in the great sacrifice. And when the pools of spilled blood finally settle, the people might see themselves in their glossy, crimson surfaces."

The first strike of the dagger finally came. And the second followed shortly after. I no longer saw Hussain. In his place, I saw Abel, Noah, Abraham, and John. But when I tried recalling my encounters with them, I remembered only Hussain. Hussain collapsed at a blow delivered to his temple by a relative. Hussain was outcasted and abused by the arrogant upper-class. Hussain gave the lives of his sons in the way of God without a moment's hesitation. Hussain would part with his blessed head at the whim of a cruel king.

And as his head slowly departed from his body, determination filled Zaynab. In the distance, she saw Kufa, Damascus, and Medina. She understood that while those lands were, at that moment, leagues away, the message she'd soon deliver to their people was sat in the very palms of her hands. That instant, the sands of Karbala shone with holy glory. Off them wafted that familiar scent of divinity. By her sides she felt the apostles of God, all of whom lived and died for this moment. Hussain's head was high on a spear, surrounded by cheers from the criminals responsible for the sight. A faint smile appeared on the face of Zaynab.

"What do you see, dear Lady?" I whispered.

Softly, Zaynab proclaimed, "I see nothing but beauty. Sacred are these blood-soaked sands and the sincere ones whose feet tread through them."

ashura: i saw nothing but beauty

Zayna Naqvi

Zayna Naqvi is a creative and artistic 12 year old with a passion for reading, writing and drawing. She loves spending time with her family and friends.

On the Day Of Ashura (the 10th of Muharram), Bibi Zaynab saw nothing but beauty because she saw her fierce 54 year old brother, Imam Hussain, the son of Imam Ali and Bibi Fatima and the grandson of Prophet Muhammad decline the paperwork of Yazid bin Mu'awiya's leadership that would now cause war. Even though Imam Hussain knew that he would die for making this decision for Islam, Imam Hussain still did it. He knew that he could not give leadership to a person like Yazid bin Muawiya because he was the son of a very cruel man and both him and his father never loved Islam or the people who kept it alive. A man that had no love for Islam could not be given leadership over people.

Another reason Bibi Zaynab saw beauty on the day of Ashura (the 10th of Muharram) was that people were dying and being killed for the sake of Imam Hussain, Allah, and Islam.

Bibi Zaynab thought that it was beautiful that Imam Hussain put his life on the line for Islam. Bibi Zaynab thought it was beautiful that everyone from any age went to fight in the battle field including Hazrat Qasim, Hazrat Ali Akbar, both her two beloved sons Hazrat Aun and Muhammad, and even the infant Hazrat Ali Asghar.

Another beautiful thing that happened on Ashura (the 10th of Muharram) is that the mothers of the young children let there beloved children go to the battlefield knowing that they would never come back to their mother's arms ever again and after their child would go, then their husband would go and they would be left with no one but the other Islamic ladies around them. Bibi Zaynab thought that was beautiful because no mother would let their children go, but for the sake of Imam Hussain the ladies let go of their spouses, children and other family members of them.

Bibi Zaynab thought on the day of Ashura (the 10th of Muharram) that it was beautiful that Bibi Sakeena, the daughter of Imam Hussain, didn't let her father know about her thirst. She did not want her father to go and get his life taken away from him. So Bibi Sakeena did not tell her father that her lips were very dry, or that she was feeling thirsty so she held her thirst and spent all her time sitting with her father for as long as she still could until it was time for him to go and fight on the battlefield.

Another beautiful thing that happened on the day of Ashura (the 10th of Muharram) was that Imam Hussain let all of his children die for the sake of Islam. Imam Hussain let his 13 year old son Ali Akbar go to the battlefield. Imam Hussain even let the last thing of his brother, Imam Hasan, go and that was the son of Imam Hasan, Qasim bin Hasan who was a young 13 year old boy killed on the battlefield . Imam Hussain also let his little 3 year old Bibi Sakeena become an orphan and die in an underground grave all alone without Bibi Zaynab with barely any food or water.

Another beautiful event that happened on Ashura (the 10th of Muharram) was that Imam Hussain brought his 6 month old baby to the battlefield to get water because the baby Ali Asghar's lips where so dry. Imam Hussain could not take it so he wrapped him in a cloak and brought him to the battle-field and Ali Asghar was shot with a three headed arrow and died. Imam Hussain still stayed strong and fought on the battle field and Bibi Zaynab found that it was very beautiful that Imam Hussain stayed strong.

Another beautiful event that happened on Ashura (the 10th of Muharram) was that Imam Hussain sacrificed all of his and his brother Imam Hasan's children for the sake of Islam. Another reason Bibi Zaynab only saw beauty on Ashura (the 10th of Muharram) was because Bibi Zaynab's two sons, Hazrat Aun and Muhammad, were only 11 and 12, but they had sacrificed their whole life for Imam Hussain. Bibi Zaynab thought that it was beautiful that her sons sacrificed their lives just for the sake of Imam Hussain and Islam. When Bibi Zaynab saw the dead bodies of her two sons Hazrat Aun and Muhammad, she thought so much of it as a sacrifice or a gift to Allah that Bibi Zaynab took out her janamaz and started praying. In her prayer, she thanked Allah for taking her two beloved sons Hazrat Aun and Muhommed back to where they came from. Bibi Zaynab thought that that was very beautiful what her sons did for the sake of Islam.

An additional beautiful event that happened on Ashura (the 10th of Muharram) was that Hazrat Abbas was the uncle of Bibi Sakeena, Ali Akbar And Ali Asghar. At one point Hazrat Abbas could not stand the sound of the hungry and the thirsty children of Islam yelling Al-Atash and asking for just one drop of water. Hazrat Abbas went to his brother Imam Hussain and asked permission to go fight on the battlefield. Imam Hussain said "I can not let you go and fight on the battlefield, but I can not either stand the voices of the children of Islam yelling out Al-Atash so I will send you to go get water. Do not go fight the people but get these get these children water." So Hazrat Abbas got his sword and went to get these thirsty children of Islam water. Bibi Zaynab found this very beautiful . Another thing she found beautiful about the day of Ashura is that Hazrat Abbas was the bravest of all the 72 companions because all his life he trained for a day like Ashura. But of all 72 companions of Imam Hussain, Hazrat Abbas was the only one that did not go and fight on the battlefield just because Imam Hussain was Hazrat Abbas's brother and leader. Hazrat Abbas listened to Imam Hussain and did not go and fight. Instead he went to River Euphoria with his water bucket and got water. As Hazrat Abbas went towards the camp both hands got cut off so he put the water bag in his teeth, but when the bag of water got pierced with an arrow Hazrat Abbas gave up and fell to the ground and yelled "BROTHER." Imam Hussain ran and brought Hazrat Abbas back to the camp to bury him. Hazrat Abbas's words were "Please don't bring me to the camp. I promised the children of Islam water, but i have none so please just leave me here. Bibi Zaynab thought it was beautiful that Hazrat Abbas went through all of this just to get the children of Islam some water to drink so they be happy.

Another beautiful event that had occurred on the day of Ashura (the 10th of Muharram) was that Hurr bin Yazid had blocked the pathway for the 72 companions and Imam Hussain so the companions and imam hussain where forced to go on the path of Karbala, where they were going to be soon martyred. Then when Hurr Bin Yazid heard the powerful mind changing speech that Imam Hussain made, he with no doubt Hurr Bin Yazid changed his mind and side. He brought his son and horse and went to the side where the Prophet's grandson and 72 companions stayed for shelter and said to the Imam "I want to be the first one to go to the battlefield and die." He did not even get off his horse to say Salam to everyone. He went straight to the battlefield and fought bravely until he finally died. Bibi Zaynab found this very beautiful.

Another beautiful event that occured on the day of Ashura (the 10th of Muharram) was that the 72 companions, and the family of Imam Hussain did not starve themselves or go to the battlefield to fight or to be murdered for themselves. They died, got murdered, and starved themselves to save the message that Prophet Muhammad got on the Cave of Hira and told his people that had been passed on to Imam Hussain to save. Bibi Zaynab found this very beautiful. Another beautiful event that occurred on the day of Ashura (the 10th of Muharram) was that when the sons of the mothers did not come back the mothers did not mothers did not give up or leave Imam Hussain's side.

They stayed strong and thanked Allah for taking their beloved sons back to where they had come from. Bibi Zaynab found that it was very beautiful that when Imam Hussain saw that his 6 month old baby Ali Asghar was so thirsty that his lips were dry he took the 6 month old baby ali Asghar and rapped him in the cloak and went to Yazid Bin Muawiyah tent and said, "This baby has done nothing to you, so please just give him a drop of water and if you don't trust me then I will leave the baby here just give him water." Besides from a few tears nobody cared so they called Hurmala Bin Kahil and then this cruel man took a three headed arrow and killed the 6 month old baby Ali Asghar. Bibi Zaynab thought this was very beautiful because no matter what happened to Imam Hussain even though his baby died he kept on trying until he succeeded.

Another beautiful event that happened on the day of Ashura (the 10th of Muharram) was that Imam Hussain's grandfather Prophet Muhammad started spreading the message so long ago, and it is beautiful that the Prophet's grandson is now fighting for the message that his grandfather started.

Another event that occured on the day of Ashura (the 10th of Muharram) was after all the men were murdered, the ladies of Islam were being slapped and being treated horribly. Bibi Sakeena was treated the most cruelest. She was put in a dark underground prison, with barely any food or barely any water. The thing Bibi Zaynab thought was the most beautiful was that Bibi Sakeena (the daughter of Imam Hussain) did not give up or did not stop believing in Islam up until she died in the dark underground prison with barely any food or water.

Another beautiful event that occurred on the day of Ashura was that Bibi Sakeena barely drank any water or ate any food because of the really cruel death of her father (Imam Hussain), her 13 year old brother Ali Akbar and her very young 6 month old baby brother, but she still had a lot of love in her for Islam and missed her family very much.

The most beautiful thing that happened on Ashura (the 10th of Muharram) that was the most important of all times it was that the people of Prophet Muhammad where saying strong on the the horrifying and very cruel day of Ashura (the 10th of Muharram).

Wait for Me in Karbala

Mohd Faizal Musa

Mohd Faizal Musa, also known under the pen name Faisal Tehrani, is an award-winning Malaysian author and playwright whose works have been read across the globe.

Munir's emerald eyes glistened. The bowl of oats he had pre-pared laid there, licked clean by me. His younger brother, Hussain sat to his side, smiling as if hiding something. I adjusted my coat and the turban curled around my neck. Last night, rain descended upon Karbala and temperatures went down sharply. Munir eventually gathered enough courage to ask, "Akhi, ente is Shi'a?"

Now it was my eyes that glossed over. I wanted to answer the way the famous Indonesian ulama, Hamka, had. Almar-hum had been to Karbala twice. He was once asked the same question. His reply, as written in the preface to the translation of Al-Hussain Bin Ali by al-Hamid al-Hussaini was, 'I am not of Shi'a mazhab, but I love Hussain!' But I caged in those early words by Hamka as I felt they meant nothing to these two. All I said was, "I love Hussain. As do the both of you. Had not Rasulullah said: 'These two are my children and the child of my daughter. Oh Allah, verily I love them both, therefore love them both and those who love them.' I seek the love of Allah, therefore I love Hasan and Hussain."

Hussain, Munir's brother, cracked a smile on his lips before laughing softly. As if I had declared my love for him. Oh, how beautiful would it be for a Sunni and a Shi'a to unite in their love for Rasulullah's grandson?

Such was my brief interaction with Munir and Hussain. They arrived in Karbala from Kazimiyyah, Baghdad as vol-unteers to receive guests of Saidina Hussain's tomb.

"Two weeks." Munir made a gesture with his fingers.

"We will clear rubbish and provide food for guests of Imam Hussain. We don't have a lot of money. But what we have, we will give for Hussain," Hussain interjected with more vigour.

Perhaps it was the gust of wind grazing my face that made me feel a rush of tenderness. Perhaps I was instantly ready to battle melancholy every time I faced the edges of the tombs of Saidina Hussain and Abal Fadz.

On the streets, mourning processions had begun since dawn. The tomb of Imam Hussain, its golden dome with the red flag on top waving listlessly, was faintly visible, shrouded by the cool of winter. Truth be told, I was slightly anxious. My laptop was confiscated by American soldiers as soon as I entered the Iraq border. I was lucky to find a room to rent. But, my favourite Nikon camera had to be left in the room in the interest of safety. Word was that on more than one occasion, explosions happened in Karbala with the use of tiny bombs hidden in cameras, cellphones and computers. So, I felt uneasy because I could not record what was expected of me as a traveller.

From before I made it past the border and into Karbala, I already asked a border guard in Kermanshah, who looked like he knew what was going on. The guard, named Redza, asked, "Brother, are you Sunni? Do you mean to say Sunan Tirmidzi?"

I did not answer. Sunni or Shi'a wasn't too important if our hearts are with Allah, the Rasul, and his family, as uttered during selawat in our prayers. The guard went on, reaching for kitab Imam Tirmidzi from his bookshelf which was stuffed to the seams. "In the Sahih Tirmidzi, hadith number 3860: Abu Said al-Asyajj narrated to us, Abu Khalid al-Ahmar told us, Razin told us, he said Salam narrated to us, he said: I went to the presence of Ummu Salamah while she was weeping and so I asked: 'What makes you weep?' She said: I saw Rasulullah in a dream and his head and beard were smeared with dust. I asked: 'What happened to you, oh Rasulullah.' He replied: 'Just now I have witnessed the murder of Al-Hussain.' People ask us, why do the Shi'a cry? I want to ask, why don't the Sunni cry? How is it that they must not cry?"

I felt small, stammering in front of a low-ranking border guard.

Redza went on to explain, "Ummu Salamah, the wife of Rasulullah pbuh herself cried when remembering the murder of Imam Hussain, why not us? The Prophet never stopped his wife. In fact, Prophet Muhammad appeared before Ummu Salamah in such despair that he was smeared with dust. Prophet Yaakub a.s mourned the loss of Prophet Yusuf until he turned blind, Allah didn't forbid this. Why are there people who ask why we cry when remembering the tragic slaughter and murder of the Prophet Muhammad's pbuh grandson. Is that not strange?"

For a while, I felt ashamed of myself. I studied Shari'a for my degree but never went into such depth. Today, after leaving the subject of Shari'a as an academic and deepening my study of comparative literature, I vowed to peel away all the layers in Shari'a. I now understand a hadith that goes:

"Mahmud bin Ghailan narrated to us, Abu Daud al Hafari narrated to us from Sufyan from Yazid bin Abu Ziyad, from Binu Abi Nu'am, from Abu Sa'id al Khudri radiallahuanhu, he said: The Prophet said, 'Hasan and Hussain are leaders of the youths of paradise.'" In my mind I grappled with the question, are there old people in paradise? If I loved Hussain as the Prophet sought, what is the proof? I didn't even know about his tragic and haunting death in detail or in its true form, so how could I confess to love him and have my heart set on occupying paradise? Isn't it true that what we don't know, we cannot love. The question then is: do I really know why Saidina Hussain, the commander of paradise, was murdered a martyr and what the philosophy was behind his great sacrifice?

When I was studying at the Kelang Islamic College, at an usrah led by a naqib I asked why Prophet Muhammad asked us to love his grandson, Saidina Hussain. The naqib, who is now a renowned ulama, answered, "It is the love of a grandfather for his grandson." Since that day I distanced myself from such false words. How could it be merely the love of a grandfather for his grandson? Prophet Muhammad is a messenger of Allah. His every word and deed is from Allah swt. 'Nor does (Prophet Muhammad) speak from his own inclination. It is but not a revelation revealed.' Such is Allah's decree in surah An Najm, verses 3 and 4.

True, Saidina Hussain was killed in Karbala by the combined treason of the people of Kufah and the cruelty of Yazid and his associates; but surely, the incident happened for a reason. Like the elements I commanded when writing fiction, plot is cause and effect. Here, the 'effect' could be seen in Karbala; the 'cause' meanwhile was in Madinah. I had just returned from Madinah, where I performed the Hajj. I witnessed a heart wrenching cause and a most tragic effect. History bears causality. Cause and effect. I needed to find it. That is why I rushed over. Immediately, I recalled the early chapters of the book, The Biggest Fitna in the History of Islam by Taha Hussain which was translated into Malay and published by Dewan Bahasa dan Pustaka in 1990.

"What brings enta here?" Husin asked, seemingly unsatisfied with my answer. My reverie stopped abruptly. Truly, I gathered the courage to cross the Iran border and come here because I was tracking down material for an acade mic book about the mourning drama (ta'ziyeh) of Imam

Husin, for comparison to the mourning of Jesus (liturgy) in the Catholic Christian denomination. In the homeland I was hurled with slanderous hearsay that I am Shi'a because of my interest in studying this obscure topic. But I had no concerns for such accusations.. Only Allah and Prophet Muhammad would assess the condition of my iman. I wouldn't be sharing a burial plot with the accusers.

Hussain suddenly quipped, "Faisal, if we truly love the Prophet, we must then celebrate his birth, observe israk misraj, celebrate every joy of Prophet Muhammad pbuh. Why is it that during Prophet Muhammad's sadness and grief we act as if we have forgotten him and do not want to shed a tear, as the Prophet himself has done? Can enta love the Prophet and only be with him during the good times and leave him when he is sad? Isn't that very strange? And it's clear, Prophet Muhammad pbuh was in grief upon the martyrdom of his grandson, who was tortured so brutally."

That afternoon, I was due to leave for Samarra. The roads were crammed with visitors in mourning while remember-ing Saidina Hussain. I worried that braving the sea of people on the roads would delay my journey towards Baghdad.

"Wait for me here, in Karbala." I said to Munir and Hus-sain. "I will be in Samarra just for the day, and will be back tomorrow."

Munir nodded. Hussain smiled. His eyes had a sheen like glass. I held Hussain's hand and opened its grip; in his palm, I placed a keychain of the Petronas Twin Towers. He hugged me, delighted. He said he wanted to save money to learn English in Kuala Lumpur. Then, Munir and Hussain gave me a framed picture. A photograph of the tombs of Imam Hasan Askari dan Hadi Naqi in Samarra that had been bombed by wahabi terrorists. I touched Hussain's shoulder,

"I will be back. Wait for me in Karbala. Here."

The two of them sent me to my taxi. Hussain cried. Munir comforted him. I fought back the lump in my throat. That night, on the way to Samarra, the taxi was stopped repeatedly at control posts. As soon as we arrived in Baghdad, the guard at a control post muttered something to the taxi driver. In my exhausted daze and inability to hear what they were saying, I paid no heed. It was only when we stopped for fajr prayers at a mosque by the side of the road that that the driver broke the news, "There was an explosion in Karbala. It happened 150 metres from the zarih of Imam Hussain. Hundreds of visitors were martyred in front of the father of all martyrs."

I performed my fajr prayers with tears streaming down my face. I prayed to Allah to protect Munir and Hussain. I wanted to see them again in Karbala. I wanted to continue the friendship. I wanted Munir and Hussain to learn English in Kuala Lumpur one day.

When I returned to Karbala later that day, I waited at the same place. They were not there. I looked for Munir and Hussain at their usual place, where they made the creamy oat porridge. A friend of theirs, Musa, with grief in his eyes, spoke to me in a mix of despair and delight.

"They have been martyred. They were killed in yesterday's explosion. And in Hussain's hand, while he clinged to the zarih of Imam Hussain, there was a keychain. The keychain that you gave him, he took it to paradise."

Oh, my grief for Hussain. My grief for Hussain. I cried endlessly that day. I still remember the day. It was the morning of the tenth of Muharram. I lost two Hussains. This Muharram marks almost a year since I got to know Munir and Hussain. My words, 'Wait for me in Karbala,' still send echoes in my heart. And I always ask, 'Why did they kill Hussain, why?'

Conference of the Forest

Batool Rizvi

Batool Rizvi is a poet, educator, and community organizer who completed her certification in Creative Writing from UCLA and her work is informed by religious and spiritual teachings.

A veiny leaf falls off a maple tree to the forest floor, joining thousands of others. A harsh wind flips it over, the silvery underside exposed to the upcoming winter.

"Umme, Umme! Look at me!"

Amena Aziz's observations are cut short as her owlet, Dena, hops from one twig to the next. Amena walks further into the hollow and caresses her two other daughters, who play with broken twigs next to each other. Cautious of her oldest daughter's ambitions, Amena warns, "Habibti Dena, careful now. Flying is still new for you."

"Watch me, watch me--" Dena sings, flapping her almost fully grown wings near the hollow's edge, ready for takeoff and oblivious to her mother's concerns.

"Dena. Wait."

Dena turns around, wing on hip, and lets out a frustrated sigh, "Umme. What?" She scrunches her face at her two younger sisters playing behind Umme. They're so young, so immature. I'm better than them. I know more than them—there's a whole world out there waiting for us and all they want to do is play with twigs.

"A few hops here and a flight there doesn't count," Amena reminds. "This is the real world. Oh, I fear you will let your curiosity get in the way. Remember: flying requires practice and patience. Are you sure you're ready?"

Dena scoffs at Umme and looks at the gray clouds looming above. Curving her beak, furrowing her eyebrows, she confidently replies, "Of course I am. I was born ready!"

Strings of prayer escape Amena's beak as she watches Dena

meet air. "Oh watch it, there's a branch to your left. Careful, there's a nest in front of you--"

"Huh? Umme, what'd you say? I can't hearrrr you!" The wind tickles the young owlet and sweeps her in a circle around a nearby branch. "WEEE! FREEDOM!"

Dena flaps her wings and tries to ascend higher. "Did you know the trees have tops and the skies go on forever and ever? I can see EastPatch from above! I love it here! I'm invincible!" She continues to point out every detail to Umme and basks in the glory. She curves her beak further, gloating as her sisters watch from below.

Dipping back down, closer to the hollow, Dena exclaims, "Hey everybody, watch me!!" With her wings fully spread out, she loops around the maple tree in front of theirs and her sisters clap and squeal. Oh how they wish they could be me! Encouraged by the cheering, Dena flies higher and hoots, "WATCH ME, WATCH MEEE--"

"COME BACK DENA! THAT'S ENOUGH FOR TODAY!" Amena speeds out of the hollow as Dena flaps her wings and flies further and further away from EastPatch, away from home.

Now, nearing the edge of the forest, Dena sees sparkling white ahead. Could this be what Umme calls 'The Beyond?' Dena looks over her shoulder. Phew. Umme is still far away.

"DON'T GO TO THE WEST SIDE OF THE FOREST!" Amena frantically yells.

"I guess not far enough," Dena grumbles to herself. But this must be The Beyond. This must be why Umme doesn't want me to enter. Dena takes in the great, white fog. It's like a shiny diamond waiting to be discovered amidst the rest of the green forest that's flanked by maple trees. This is it, I've finally discovered it!

"WEEEEE!! WATCH ME FLY-- "

"NOOO DENAAA--"

A chorus of cries echoes across the forest floor. An orchestra of crickets and wasps gasp in harmony. Thousands of maple leaves rustle. The wind howls, shedding leaves from their trees. It's like a blanket of brown covering the ground. Perhaps to cancel the noise. Perhaps to cushion the young owlet's landing.

"DENA, DENA. HABIBTI, WHERE ARE YOU? DENA!?" Amena desperately calls for her owlet but to no avail.

She flaps her wings and reaches the maple tree where she last saw Dena. She flew this way, I'm sure of it! Frantically climbing into the hollow, Amena looks around and throws brown leaves and red twigs out of her path. Empty. Where could she have gone? Surely she wouldn't have flown too far!

Amena zooms out and flies further west, towards the direction of The Beyond – a part of the forest that she made strictly off-limits, especially to her children. Surely Dena wouldn't have entered, knowing everything.

Amena stops herself right before the permanent, blinding fog engulfs her. Mother's melodious hooting. Her smile, her laughter. Tears stream down Amena's large hazel eyes as memories of her childhood resurface. Mother's cries. The separation. The hawk that stole happiness. Amena winces– it's as though she can still hear her mother's agonizing cries for help. It's as though she can still see the red drops on the cold, winter floor leading Amena to this same exact spot, twenty-two years ago. How agonizing, how painful was that separation!

She squints at the world beneath as her eyes adjust to the veil of vapor. Surely Dena remembers the stories of how her grandmother never made it out of here. How hawks and other foes dwell on this side. Surely, surely, she remembers. The same sinking feeling settles inside the pit of Amena's stomach as it did all those years ago. Only this time it's worse. This time there is no hawk. There is only her owlet's curiosity and desire. Amena could have stopped her, she should have done more.

"HOOOT, HOOOT, HOOT!" Amena yells with her beak in the air, as a hopeless attempt to hear her daughter. She pauses to listen for at least a stirring, for some movement. But all she hears is the soft patter of snow falling and settling on the surface of maple branches.

Amena flies to another tree and enters the hollow. Empty, again. For days, she searches every nest and hollow in the vicinity of The Beyond, asks every owl she meets, and descends to land for any sign of return. But it is as though Dena no longer exists. It is as though Amena is reliving her mother's separation, only this time she doesn't know if her child is alive – if she is, then will Dena be ready for the trials ahead?

***

Dena lands on a thin sheet of leaves near the edge of a frozen lake – the foyer into The Beyond. Its visage gleams as a tiny sliver of sunlight hits at just the right angle.

She tries to lift her right wing, her lower lip quivering at its weight. Oh no! I fell! Dena swallows a whimper. Surely, I'll bounce back in no time! After all, I am invincible! For now, I'll just stay put. Looking around, she takes in her surroundings. There's white everywhere, for as far as Dena can see. White snow surrounds the frozen lake, like a cushion supporting a newborn's head. A fog blocks Dena's vision into what lies beyond the lake. Trees are sparse. She can't tell where the clouds meet the earth. Day and night seem to be one here.

"What peace! Why didn't I come to The Beyond sooner? I should never have listened to Umme and her stories about grandmother!" Dena tells herself as she tries settling into her new environment.

The foolish owlet doesn't realize that the snow on the ground actually absorbs her voice; she overlooks the bare maze of maple trees that provide little comfort; and she fails to recognize the temperature is about 20 degrees colder here than it is back in her hollow.

Deafened by the eeriness and overcome by the adrenaline of her fall, Dena doesn't pick up on someone lurking behind one of the few maple trees nearby. She doesn't see the corner of a fox's lips turning upwards in a sly grin as he mischievously thinks, Ah, yes, you should never have listened to Umme. Stay right there you foolish owlet!

Dena looks to the lake on her left. It gleams under the last few rays of sunshine. Soon, the sun will start its voyage, dip beneath the horizon, and kiss the earth. Soon, the moon will ascend, the stars will scatter like glitter, and the sky will be covered in a vast blue. I'm sure Umme will want me home but oh I just can't wait to discover what else is out here! I want to travel and see everything, and I don't need Umme or my sisters for it. I can take care of myself, I'm sure of it!

This Beyond doesn't seem so bad anyways.

Meanwhile the fox licks his lips, Ah perfect, perfect. An injured owlet! Just what I need. This is wonderful indeed! No longer able to contain his excitement, the fox lunges forward. His claws barely scratch Dena's wings.

"AHH! WHA-" He hears the owl scream, clearly taken aback. Snickering, Well at least she's distraught. Now if I could just get this annoying thing off of me. He looks up and sees the charcoal-gray, round ears of an elephant. He couldn't be more than about nine feet tall, Hah! How small for an elephant. Oh, this should be fun.

The fox locks eyes with his hostage-taker and flashes his teeth. "Right. Well if you would just let me go and I'll be on my way." His eagerness doesn't go unnoticed.

"I don't think we've met. I'm Samir." The elephant introduces himself as he holds the fox with his trunk and brings him to eye level. For a moment, the wind pauses and the snow comes to a standstill. In a deathly quiet manner Samir adds, "And you'll be on your way into the outskirts of The Beyond. Where you're meant to be."

The fox, trying to cover his squirms in the trunk's hold, smirks, "Oh you are so full of passion. Loyalty even. But I know your kind. The great old 'Sun Herd,' ah, isn't that right?"

Samir's eyes flashes as he hears his herd's name, but instantly fall back as the fox continues, "You will never eat me. You lot walk around priding yourselves as the engineers of The Beyond, of this side of the forest. I admire that, really, I do."

The fox catches a glimpse of the owl and sees her trying to lift her right wing.

This is my chance, this is my chance. C'mon giant elephant, let me go!

Chuckling, the fox starts again, "But tell me, uh, Samir, was it?"

Samir squints his eyes then nods. What is this fox up to?

Chuckling again, the fox goes for the kill, "Right. Samir, tell me this: does your height, compared to the other herds, make you feel inferior? Is that why you resort to such pathetic labels? Do they make you feel all mighty and noble?" Laughing hysterically now, then spitting on the snow, the fox challenges, "How dare you think someone like me will be afraid of someone like you?"

Steam comes out of Samir's round ears as he hears this indecent behavior. But he remains calm, he was taught better, "You know what they say about Samir?" The elephant pauses looking directly into the fox's eyes.

For a moment, the snow yearns to melt. The trees wish to disintegrate. Dena whines behind the duo – how could the fox do this to me? Especially when I was about to embark on my adventure? How will I travel? Hearing the fox's cynical laughter, she looks up. She tries not to whimper and bites down her tongue. I don't know if I can take this pain.

"They say don't mess with Samir." Inhaling deeply, he lets out a loud trumpet that could have cracked the fog surrounding the lake. "AND DON'T YOU DARE DISTURB THE YOUNGINS OF THIS FOREST AGAIN. I WILL GET THE WHOLE CONFERENCE, THE WHOLE KINGDOM,

TO TURN ON YOU. I WILL TELL HIM ABOUT YOU."

Samir swings his trunk back with might, the fox's eyes widening in fear with each added inch. Samir catapults the fox deep into the whiteness that swallows him like a black hole. The trees breathe a sigh of relief, their branches calmly fall back into place, and their leaves gingerly settle to the forest floor.

Turning around, Samir gently approaches the whimpering figure, "Are you wounded young owlet?"

Dena eyes the giant elephant. Hmm, should I tell him the truth? If I tell him I didn't listen to Umme, and landed here and hurt my wings, that will make me look like a fool. I should just blame the fox. Nodding her head, "I was just admiring the lake and the snow, then got surprise attacked. The fox got me! I probably won't be able to fly for a while. Argh, and that means I won't be able to travel and explore! I'll probably have to stay here and rest and–" Dena pauses and huffs in annoyance.

The corner of Samir's eyes crinkle as he smiles kindly. "I know I am a stranger but a wise person once told me that those who make up stories end up regretting it later."

Dena looks up sheepishly. "I--OW" She hoots as pain shoots up her right wing and consumes her once again. It becomes sharper and less numbed by the adrenaline of the initial fall. Should I have listened to Umme? Should I have stopped when she told me to? I never would have been in this dilemma.

"I want to help and return you home but--"

"Home?!? Who said anything about home?!" Dena exclaims,

squinting as a couple tears betray her and pool by her talons. The drops melt the snow below her, leaving tiny gaps on the surface. *Should I go home?! I'll surely be a laughingstock! Should I have shown off my wings? Have I gone too far?*

"I feel as though you aren't telling me the full story of what happened, but maybe you can after I take you to meet someone who I know will heal your injured wing."

Dena scoffs, "And who is this, some sort of magician?"

Samir ignores the sarcasm and patiently explains, "Why would I take you to a magician? Did you hear what the fox said earlier? I pride myself in being from the Sun herd. We are the engineers of the west side of the forest and we have an unspoken pact with the rest of the creatures. We, I, vow to keep our ecosystem safe and help others in need. This way of life has been passed down from our ancestors and we take it very seriously. As children, we are taught to be selfless and sacrifice ourselves for others. Do you understand?"

Dena had wondered why the elephant didn't just leave her earlier. She was sure that if the tables were reversed, she probably would've left. *He did save me from the fox.* "Oh alright, take me to this magician."

"He's not a magician."

"Okay."

"He's more like a healer."

"Whatever you say."

"Hey I never asked you, what's your name?"

from behind. "WATCH OUT!"

Samir moves as fast as he can to the right side of the path just as a team of horses gallops past them. Their hooves click on the earth and dust kicks in the air, creating mini tornadoes. Dena can barely see in front of her. Samir yells, "Dena, are you alright up there?"

"Yes! I'm fine, I'm fine! Are you?"

"Yes I am, thank you! But don't worry about me."

Just as the two catch their breath, they hear a clip-clop, clip-clop, clip-clop approaching them. A stunning horse with fur as white as snow, a wedge-shaped head, large brown eyes, a small muzzle, and a long neck, stops before them. Dust around him, he looks like a stunning Arabian prince from a painting.

"Samir, my old friend! I hope we did not cause a fright. If we did, I do apologize." The horse politely bows his head to Samir, then Dena.

"Oh, no worries. Appreciate the warning, I knew that voice sounded familiar!" Samir raises his eyes to his head, "Dena, this is my dear friend, Uqab, we've been

friends since we were born."

Samir looks to Uqab, "How are you dear friend?"

"Praise the Lord, I have no complaints. We were just racing but I think I've had enough for today. I don't want my coat to be all messed up. How about you, what are you up to?"

"Oh we are just coming from the lake, Uqab meet Dena.

"Dena. Dena Aziz."

"Well, Dena Aziz, it's a pleasure and I'm glad to be of service. My name is Samir."

"Yes yes, Samir, Sun Herd, forest pact, being nice. Got it. Maybe I should try that, it would've saved me from this mess." Uh-oh! Did I say that out loud?

She watches in horror, beak wide open, as Samir raises his eyebrows, puzzled.
Oh no, I did!

He watches Dena bicker with herself and reassures her, "It's okay, Dena, it's okay."

She looks up; now it's her turn to be confused. In a small voice she asks, "You won't ask me why I should be nicer?"

"I'm sure whatever brought you to the foyer of The Beyond happened for a reason. I've learned that what you need will always find its way to you." He smiles confidently.

Dena stays quiet for the first time and lets his words sink in. Hmm, maybe I will get to travel. Maybe I need this magi–I mean healer.

She allows Samir to take her in his trunk and is tenderly placed on top of his head, in between his ears. Instantly, her wings ease and her eyes relax.

Samir tries to look up at Dena but all he can see is her beak pointing in the air, "We have a bit of a journey ahead of us before we meet him. I'm sure we'll become good friends!"

The pair slowly make their way around the periphery of

the frozen lake, walking amidst the fog. Dena slides from side to side on Samir's head, chuckling as his ears tenderly embrace her. Her breath steams in the air as she barters her warm laugh with the chilled droplets enveloping them.

The fog clears up and Dena feels a vibration in her heart. It's as though nothing will be the same. She sees they have reached a black gate.

"Ooh, this feels haunted." Dena whispers. "West Entrance to The Beyond" she gasps reading the sign. Umme's Umme must have been brought here all those years ago and eaten by the hawk! "Uhhh…Samir, are you sure you know where we're going?"

"Of course young Dena, have no fear, Samir is here! I know this forest backwards and forwards and side to side."

The two cross the threshold. There's no looking back now. Pretty soon, the whiteness of the sky is completely covered by a thicket of trees and a canopy of vines overhead.

"This seems similar to EastPatch, the part of the forest I grew up in!" Dena tells Samir. But here only a glimmer of sunlight passes through, in between the empty spaces of the twisting vines above.

Dena presses her talons into Samir's head, making sure he's still there.

"Ow!"

"What?"

"You just pressed your talons into my skull!"

"No I didn't." Dena lies.

"Yes, you–" Samir starts, but then softly asks, "Are you afraid?"

"Why would I be afraid? I'm never scared. I'm always up for an adventure! And finally I'm here in The Beyond! No rules, no Umme, I can do whatever I want!" Dena feigns laughter, partly nervous he won't buy it, and partly guilty for telling lies to cover up her fear. He doesn't seem like he would mock me if I admitted being a little bit scared.

Samir stops and looks above at her beak. "Sorry to burst your bubble, but there are rules. Even here."

"Of course there's rules, of course you'd make sure to enforce them," Dena remarks. "Also, why is there no one else here besides us?"

"Oh, that's all that you see. If only you could see what I see." Samir stares at a space in front of the trees ahead, almost in a trance, while Dena shifts uncomfortably above.

"What do you mean?" She chuckles nervously.

"You will know with time Dena, do not fret. I should warn you that this path can be a bit dangerous, especially for those who have never journeyed to The Beyond before. But there are only two rules here: be patient and be willing to learn."

"Why do you always speak in a puzzle? I have to piece everything together myself."

Samir comes out of his trance and starts moving again, the two now deeper into the forest. They hear a rumble coming

The sly fox injured her. I am taking her to meet the healer, the only man who can treat her wings. I know he will help." Samir and Uqab exchange a look of understanding as Uqab nods in certain agreement.

He turns to Dena and declares, "I am Uqab the fourteenth, from the Uqab team. The man Samir is taking you to, I've met many times. He will surely help. He is a true healer."

"That's what Samir says." Dena says, "So, your team is named after you?"

A proud smile adorns his sculpted face. "Oh, well, it is far more complicated than that. The team was originally named in memory of one of my ancestors. Several great grandfather's ago, there was a horse who was originally named Murtajiz. But he was later given the name Uqab, which means Eagle. He only had one son, whom he named Uqab the second, and from there the cycle repeated. So I am named after him and my son will be Uqab the fifteenth, carrying the name as well."

"Why don't you join us? I always enjoy hearing this story, and I'm sure he would love to see you too! But let's remember, to not let vanity and fame become obstacles in our paths." Samir gently reminds his friend.

Uqab lowers his gaze in guilt, "Yes dear Samir. I am working on it."

"Not to fret, not to fret. I'm sure with time you will overcome any shortcomings." Samir kindly smiles at Uqab.

The trio moves further along the dust path. Vines fall from the canopy above, making it difficult to see in front of them.

"So, who was your grandfather, and what made him so famous for a whole team to be named after him?" Dena looks down eagerly at Uqab. Samir sighs at the question. What did I just say?

"He was a legend who was part of famous battles, and superior to other horses." Samir clears his throat. "Not because of his looks or accomplishments, but rather because of his morals. Samir here always reminds me of that. It's a V.I.P."

"A VIP?" Dena scrunches her beak. "Like a Very Important Person?"

Samir chuckles, as Uqab and Samir say in unison, "A Very Important Point."

"Okay..."

"Dena, you will learn Samir has many VIPs – like rules and points about being patient and learning..." Uqab trails off.

"He already told me those."

"Alright, tease me but I'm telling you, VIPs come in handy!" Samir laughs.

"Continue with your story Uqab."

"Right, so anyways humans and animals started hearing about Uqab the first's accomplishments, and slowly my grandfather became famous. The healer we're about to see also knows my grandfather, and he always reminds me that although Uqab the first was famous, he was never running after fame. I guess, because I'm always chasing fame, the healer sends my buddy Samir here, who is always there to remind me of this VIP."

Uqab pauses in front of a puddle to check his reflection. He stares at his white coat and fixes his mane. "Anyways, to know my grandfather, I would have to tell you about one of his riders, who is actually the healer's uncle. What loyalty he had! They say my grandfather was great, but I think this rider made him greater and reach infinite heights. The rider was the true legend, the real hero. He was the son of the lion of God - he was Abbas bin Ali. Abbas was like the moon who orbited the sun. And, my goodness, what a sun – his older brother al-Husayn. How lucky was my grandfather to have served the great three – Mohamad, Ali, and Abbas, the noble men of the AhleBayt." Uqab gallops a few steps ahead of Samir and Dena, as if to add dramatic effects, and whispers, "How lucky, how famous."

"There's that fame again Uqab!" Samir reminds his friend.

"Right, right, sorry." Uqab shakes his muzzle. "Forget about the fame, Dena, remember good morals take you a long way. It's a VIP I'm trying to constantly remember."

Dena, enthralled by the story, continues with her questions: "What happened to Uqab the first, and his rider Abbas?"

Uqab sharply turns around and withdraws a breath. "There was a battle." He chokes and looks down as large, globular tears flow from the corners of his almond eyes and trickle down his cheeks.

"There, there my friend." Samir comforts Uqab.

Dena looks down, silent and unsure what to do. It was like witnessing a stunning painting stuck in a fractured frame.

Uqab looks up and inhales, continuing with his story, "It was known as the tragedy of Kerbala. In a land far, far away from here." Uqab's eyes drift to the sky, looking through the gaps in the vines. "On the tenth of the month of Muharram, known as Ashura, destinies were changed. The moon that had once orbited the sun, that had once blessed the earth, ascended back to the skies. The moon is the Qamar Bani-Hashim, Abbas son of Ali, who departed, and with him so too did the sun."

By now, Samir also has tears in his eyes. Dena feels her heart vibrating again. The same feeling she had as they entered the West Entrance to The Beyond – a heaviness she cannot explain. She follows Samir's and Uqab's gaze, and looks up through the vines, at the sky. What a sight it was: the sun and the moon, for a moment together! But just as quickly, the sun melts away, finally. The frozen lake in the distance glimmers blue as the moon reflects the sun's light, taking its position.

"Every morning and every night I come to this same spot so I can witness this dialogue. At sunrise the sun mourns the moon's departure, at sunset the moon mourns the sun's departure." Uqab takes a final glance and looks back at Dena, then Samir.

Dena sees the pain in his eyes. No, there's no way he can be making this up.

"What happened to Abbas? What about Husayn? Why did they depart? What happened to your grandfather at this battle?" Dena, in a rush of trying to get answers, forgets the pain in her right wing and hops up on Samir's head, just to fall back down. "Ugh! My wing! How far until we reach this healer?"

Samir reminds Dena, "Remember the VIPs of The Beyond-- be patient and willing to learn. We will be there in due time." Samir seems to know something Dena does not. She sighs, but remains silent. Samir, in a softer tone, looks at the path in front of them and then to Uqab, "Uqab, are you ready to start moving again?"

Uqab wipes his eyes, though Dena sees no tears, and says, "Oh Samir, you know me." Uqab shakes his head, "Let's walk faster so we can reach the healer quickly. Dena, he can answer all of your questions much more eloquently than I can--"

But before Uqab finishes they suddenly hear a cry in the distance, like that of a gazelle's. "Ahh! What is that?" Dena tries to stop the horrible sound by covering her ears with her left wing. "It won't stop!"

Samir looks up, and trumpets loudly in response to the cry, as a sign to the gazelle. "We must take the path to the right, where the cry is coming from!" The three look to the path on the right - almost complete darkness.

"But the path on the left at least has some moonlight, and seems less dark." Dena observes.

"No, that is out of the question. I helped you when you were wounded, now we must help the gazelle!" Samir is determined.

"Okay, I guess you're right Samir." Dena looks at her wounded wing and feels ashamed.

The cry seems higher-pitched now. "Ooh, oh, Samir, should I run to catch her? Should I?" Uqab looks ready to gallop, eager to be the hero.

"No, we must be cautious and stay close together." Samir

looks at Uqab then at Dena's beak, above him. "There may be other creatures lurking, waiting for one of us to become vulnerable. I fear the same may have happened to the gazelle."

"How are you so sure? Is it that whole you can see but I can't see thing?" Dena pries, trying to find answers, but Samir stays silent.

Uqab, though a little defeated, stays close behind Samir, while Dena holds on to his round elephant ears. Samir stays calm and patient, watchful for anyone who might be look-ing to attack. It is as though they are walking into a room with blindfolds on. Only a tiny speck of light, the size of a dime, seems to be at the end of the pathway. Little do they know, the end is actually miles away.

Ssss Sssss Ssssss.

Dena shrieks. "S-s-snake," she says shakily, pointing above as Samir and Uqab follow her talon. They see a pair of blue-gray eyes glowing in the dark. Suddenly, a wave of blue washes above them, countless eyes staring down. The canopy of vines overhead turns into a canopy of poisonous green snakes hissing at them.

"Be patient. Do not frighten them and they will not attack you." Samir states calmly.

"Frighten them? What about them frightening us?" Dena whispers.

"Who says we are frightened?" Samir smiles.

"What do you mean? How can you not be?" Dena asks dumbfounded.

"Dena, we must have trust like Abbas and al-Husayn, like the moon does for the sun and the sun for the moon. That one will rise once the other falls and the cycle continues. We must have patience like the sun and the moon. This is a VIP."

Dena looks wide-eyed at Samir then Uqab, who stares at her. He smiles as she starts to piece together Samir's puzzle of VIPs. "It's okay Dena, I'm also learning" Uqab reassures her.

"Now let's go to that gazelle. Be careful and hold on." Samir moves forward, careful to not touch the snakes. They move as fast as possible, with the sound of the gazelle's cry guiding them. Finally they reach her as the crying becomes intolerable, like a child incessantly wailing for its mother.

"OH GAZELLE IS THAT YOU? I AM SAMIR FROM THE SUN HERD. I HAVE COME WITH MY FRIENDS. WE WANT TO HELP, WHERE ARE YOU?" Samir trumpets above the noise of the gazelle's cries and the snakes' hissing.

The gazelle stops crying as she senses that Samir is near.

Dena wonders, Does the gazelle also feel Samir's soothing presence like I did once I sat on his head?

"Yes, yes it's me, Gazelle." Gazelle whimpers. "I'm to your left, stuck in these vines! I was going back to my children but the snakes deceived me into entering this path, saying this way was faster. Oh, how I fear history repeating itself!"

Dena spots Gazelle, "Samir, there, to our left! She's stuck!"

"Great job Dena, thank you for helping!" Samir encourages her and she smiles happy to be of assistance.

"Gazelle, what do you mean history is repeating itself?" Dena questions.

"Oh well you see, my great-great-great-great-great-great-great-great-great-great-great- great-great-grandmother was in the same predicament thousands of years ago. Except instead of vines and snakes, her feet were bound in a rope. A hunter trapped her. She was also on her way to her children."

"Oh no! What happened?" Dena asks, worried.

"Well, have you all heard of the healer?" Gazelle looks at the three of them.
Samir and Uqab look at each other, then at Gazelle. "Yes, we have."

"Again with the healer! What about him, Gazelle?" Dena does not bring up how much she wishes to meet him now. VIPs: Be patient. Learn.

"Well the healer's great-great grandfather, known as Ali bin Musa, freed my grandmother!"

"No way! What happened?" Uqab questions.

"He pleaded with the hunter to release my grandmother so she could feed her hungry fawns. He guaranteed her against the hunter and stayed in the forest as a hostage until her return. When the hunter saw that my grandmother came back, along with her fawns, and surrendered herself, he immediately freed her and apologized to Ali bin Musa."

"Woah, and where did she go after that?" Dena asks.

"Hmm, I'm actually not sure. Maybe if I get out of this alive and meet the healer, I could ask him. He can even teach me a thing or two about bravery. Because I need it!"

"Oh, I'm sure you're brave." Uqab defends.

"But I'm not. Not like my grandmother, not like all of you. I don't have wings, I don't have a large trunk, I can't run in these vines, save me, save me! It's nighttime, my kids are probably worried without me!"

"Gazelle, listen, we'll get you out of here safely. You'll meet your children, just have faith and stay patient. That's the only way we can get through this." Samir reassures.

"I thought the other rule was that you have to be willing to learn." Dena chimes in.

"That's correct, good job again Dena!" Samir smiles, happy she remembered.

Gazelle nods her head, though no one can see it in the dark. "Yes, yes, anything for my children!"

"Okay boss, so what's the plan? I say we cut the vines with my hooves. If the snakes get mad, I'll fight them off!" Uqab, once again, was eager to save the day. "People might even remember me from this! I might become famous!" Uqab adds as an afterthought.

"Oh I don't think it's just the snakes you'll anger. There's a pack of feral wolves that I've heard roaming around here every so often. I think the snakes and the wolves want to eat me! Once I no longer heard them, I started crying and then you all showed up. I didn't think anyone heard me. But the wolves will probably hunt us if you cut these vines." Gazelle hurriedly explains.

Uqab's certainty fades away, "W-w-wolves?"

Samir contemplates the new information given. "Hmm… The pack might be coming back soon. Okay, Uqab how fast can you run?"

"Very fast." Uqab smirks.

"Good. Start cutting the vines."

As soon as the first vine is cut, they hear the snakes Ssss Sssss Ssssss, this time louder, like a final warning.

"They're probably alerting the wolves!" Samir exclaims. Uqab cuts the vines as fast as he possibly can. I will be the hero. The snakes slither down from the canopy down to their faces, surrounding each of them.

"They're going to choke us!" Dena yells as Gazelle is cut free.

"Oh thank you, thank you, thank you!" Gazelle cries.

"Gazelle, are you hurt? Can you run, and run fast?" Samir talks quickly, "Otherwise, I'll tie you to Uqab's back and he can run--"

"No, no I'm fine, I can run--"

"My back?--"

Samir looks back on the path they just came from. He sees four silhouettes, and hears low growling.

He looks at Uqab, "Listen, Uqab. Take Dena on your back and Gazelle you follow them closely. Run straight to the direction of the light at the end of the path, it's a bit longer but you'll make it." Samir talks loudly, over the hissing from above, which now sounds like a deafening whistle.

"Samir, what are you saying? We're a team--"

"No, listen. Uqab you're the faster of the two of us, and you all need to meet the healer. I've told you the path you must take. It's up to all of you to take it." The wolves' growls get louder, closer. "If this is where we say our goodbyes then let us accept fate. I don't mind acting like a shield, it was never about fame for me, it was always to serve." He looks at each of their faces. "Find the healer, find him."

All of a sudden the hissing stops. It's time. Samir looks at Dena, Gazelle, and finally Uqab. He quickly transfers Dena to Uqab, before anyone can protest further. "RUN AND DON'T STOP. DON'T LOOK BACK! VIP, THIS IS A VIP! GO! NOW!"

In a frenzy, the horse, the deer, and the owlet make their escape, towards the light. They couldn't have run more than a few miles when they hear a wolf's growl and an elephant trumpeting, bellowing, as if ripping the skies open. The three, though Samir warned not to, turned around and watched: a bright light, like the sun's ray, penetrates the snake canopy and the sky. It was like Samir's soul was uniting with his master's.

The three – Dena, Uqab, and Gazelle – pause to remember their guide, their friend, Samir.

"He knew the secrets of this world, and maybe even those of other worlds." Uqab cries, remembering his dear friend. Dena nods, agreeing, and lets a silent sob escape. "He was there when no one else was. He saved my life." She looks up at the two of them. Samir's constant friendly reminders about fame and vanity to Uqab, and his determination to take the dark path to stop Gazelle's screams. "No. He saved all of us. He served all of us." Serve, serve, I heard that before.

Suddenly, Dena's eyes flash as she remembers the fox and Samir at the frozen lake. "Service. Sacrifice. Selflessness. He died doing what he meant to do."

"You're right Dena. He gave us his life." Uqab agrees.

Gazelle nods as tears fall down. "But now we must honor his last VIP."

The three look ahead at the bright light, it seems larger now like the size of a door.

"We shouldn't stop. Samir told us to keep moving forward." Dena says.

The deer and the horse gallop and jump, now faster than before, all eager to make it out of the snake canopy and the wolf chase.

They reach closer to the white light. Tranquility overtakes all three of them. But there is something else. A heartache.

"Are one of you singing, or reciting something?" Dena asks Uqab and Gazelle. They shake their heads no.

"I hear that too. It's beautiful." Gazelle slows down.

The words become clearer with each step:

O Abbas, O Abbas, O Abbas.

Gallant was he, in between arrows and spears.
How can a lion be tamed? Unlike any of his peers
Abbas soars on Uqab, eagle splashes in Euphrates. "Have no fear,
Put your muzzle in the water. Quench your thirst, loyal Uqab!" Cries
Of parched children travel from the tents to here. Husayn's daughter is near.
"How should I drink when children are thirsty?" Uqab tears
His desires, Uqab is eagle of his nafs. Abbas cheers,
"This is our victory!" Waterskin full, facing God's enemies, sheer
Courage is Abbas. Sheer loyalty unsheathed. The lion roars.
Is it unclear --

Uqab gallops faster towards the light, "Who are you? Where are you? O grandfather, is that you?"

The trio reaches the bright door. No more hissing, no more wolves, no more EastPatch, no more hollow.

Dena looks in front of her, it was not what she was expecting. She thought it would be white fog, like the frozen lake where she first met Samir. But this, this seems like an extension of the forest. Every tree is lighter, every creature is brighter. The clouds parted, the night left. The sun's rays gleam and kiss Dena's face. She feels alive. Looking around it seems like a gathering of sorts, like a conference of the forest. It is as though the whole kingdom is gathered – every animal, creature, and insect under the sun. To the right are a group of deer, hushed with watery eyes. To the left are a herd of elephants trumpeting as if they have lost a beloved. I wonder if Samir belonged to the same herd. In the middle are a team of horses, with large brown eyes and beautiful white fur, neighing in grief. Tilting her head above, Dena looks to the top of the maple and oak trees. They seem to be bending in unusual ways, as if reaching their branches towards the gathering in mourning.

In the center is a wooden stump where a man in black clothing recites an elegy. Dena realizes it is the same voice the three had heard when running to the light. The man recites the end, louder now, beating his chest. Tears flow down his face, like a river ashamed of the killing of a thirsty water-bearer on its banks.

"Is that Ali in Siffin? Is that Abbas in Kerbala? Let the arrows pierce,
Let the arms fall, let the water pour. "Master, how do you crawl? It appears
A man without support, heading back to the banks. Call for Husayn, call for the Amir.
Master, Uqab calls upon you. Where shall I go? Is there life after you? My years
Illuminated by the moon reflecting the sun. Where will I go? Shall I disappear
Into mourning, forever? Entrusted to you. Victory was here, victory was you
O Abbas, O Abbas, O Abbas.'"

All the animals are encapsulated by his words. Dena closes her eyes and tries to forget the day's events. She slowly melts into the powerful hum of the elegy. At the end, her eyes flash open. She looks next to her. Salty tears pour out of Gazelle. Uqab clicks his hooves, crying. "He's talking about my grandfather, Dena. About Abbas, his rider." Dena remembers the story Uqab told her back in The Beyond; it feels like ages ago now.

This heartache, this crying, this letting go, like when leaves fall from their branches, is beautiful. This is the sacred agreement between all life. And the forest is overtaken by a melodious symphony.

Some of the creatures start to scatter, perhaps going back home. The man reciting, sets his glasses down and wipes his tears with a handkerchief. "That's him, that's the healer." Uqab points out.

At the same moment, the healer looks up at the three of them, "Ah, just in time. I was expecting you. How was your journey Dena and Gazelle? And Uqab, always a pleasure to see you. Hope you're well and not chasing fame. Your grandfather became a master controlling his own desires, you know."

"Yes it was quite a journey, but we made it. Thank you for asking, and always appreciate the reminder." Uqab bows while responding, while Dena and Gazelle stare in awe of how he knew their names.

"And how is your wing?" He nods to Dena's right side.

"How did you know?" She blurts out, then looks down ashamed at her desire to know all the answers immediately. Be patient and willing to learn. Samir's voice rings in her head.

"Oh, I can see that which you cannot. All the veils have been lifted from me."

Dena shivers. Samir once said something similar. "You are a healer."

The man chuckles, and then recites a few more verses:

"Will the caged owl fly? Like Buraq
Carried the weight of Muhammad,
Will the owl carry her weight?

Weightless, let go, shed
The ego. Ascend to the seventh sky.

Let go, let go. Desires haunt you.
Gazelle flee — the hunter of death is always near.
Have no fears, you were always brave.
God is always near. God was always here.

Dena, I always remember the Battle of Kerbala. It took place because the evil tyrant at the time, Yazid bin Muawiyyah, was mad that Husayn, my great-grandfather, did not pledge his support to him. Husayn is famous for saying, 'How can a man like me give allegiance to a man like you?' Humiliated and angry, Yazid forced Husayn and his close family members, including Abbas, to leave their home in Medina. It was heartbreaking because this was where they grew up and they had to leave all their cherished childhood memories behind. Yazid, unable to let go of his desire for power and fame did the least courageous thing: he commanded that Husayn, his family, and his companions be killed.

Eventually, with a small caravan of 72 companions, Husayn, his family, and his friends reached the desert known as Kerbala. Here was the epic faceoff between light versus darkness, truth versus falsehood. One side stood up for morality with complete faith, while the other had no morality, no character. One side, thirsty and hungry, while the other side with bellies full of the world's material riches. Eventually there came a time when Abbas, who was the flag-bearer in Husayn's army, rode with Uqab into the battlefield. And the rest, I've narrated in the elegy you heard in the gathering. Remember Abbas and his horse Uqab the first. They let go of their desire to drink water and the riches of this world. You must learn to let go of your own ego in exchange for gaining eternal peace and eternal riches."

Dena, shocked and speechless, almost feels weightless. A veil seems to be lifted, her heart expands and she seems to see clearly. "I should have listened to Umme. I should never have shown off. My sisters, though young, have their own value. I should have more patience, just like what Samir said." She flaps her wings. The answer was, and always will be within myself! What a fool I was!

"Where did she go after that?" Dena's thoughts are cut off and she turns back to look at Gazelle, who still carries tears in her eyes. "Where did my grandmother go after Ali bin Musa saved her? I want to be brave, like her." She stares directly at the healer, knowing he has the answer.

"A group of owls that were present during Ashura, flew away after the tragedy. They wanted to find a place where they could mourn and remember the incident for all of eternity. Eventually, they found The Beyond, but they were unsure of how to proceed, so they went back to tell the Sun herd."

Looking up at the skies, as if he was talking to Samir, the healer continues, "The Sun herd, that is Samir's herd, were essentially the first settlers in the West side of The Beyond. His ancestors paved the ecosystem and laid the foundation. They were, are, the bright light from which all other creatures and tribes flourish here. They make everyone else better because of their service and vow to this land." He continues looking up as a sunray glows brighter, kissing his face. "I'll see you soon, old friend." The healer whispers.

Looking back at the group he watches each closely, "I believe Samir sacrificed himself so that you could all reach me. I'm sure his sacrifice was not in vain."
Dena gulps, feeling a sense of responsibility. He's right. I owe it to Samir and everything he stood for.

Clearing his throat, the healer continues, "Following right after, came Uqab the first, and eventually his team grew. Uqab the first was looking for a place to mourn his beloved rider, Abbas bin Ali, after the events that took place at Kerbala. He found this patch of land and became friends with the Sun herd. He shared with them the story of what took place. "

Turning towards Gazelle, the healer adds, "Last came the al-Zamin herd, meaning guarantor. They were named in honor of Ali bin Musa. Gazelle, you see, your great grandmother found her way into the west side of The Beyond. It was because of her determination to keep my grandfather, Husayn's memory alive, especially after Ali bin Musa saved her and her children's life, that allowed the mourning to continue years and years after the Battle of Kerbala took place.

Do you all see it? Samir the first, Uqab the first, and Gazelle the first were all guided here. Elephants, horses, gazelles, and even the owls, used to mourn and remember the tragedy of Kerbala together. Eventually, as the herds and teams grew, so did each of their responsibilities. Now, there are so many of them that it's too hard to congregate, or many are unaware of what occurs beyond that white lit door. Much like you Gazelle, and you Dena, before you were invited here.

Gazelle, you are brave, it is only death in this life that you should fear. Uqab, you have the capacity to chase after faith, not fame. And Dena, your wings were never wounded when you fell; it was only your ego and your heart that were bruised. You could always fly, in this world and the next. Fly Dena, fly."

Dena looks up at the sky. The sun, ever-bright. An owl is

circling in the air, as if lost, not knowing she is found. With a newfound strength, Dena begins flapping her wings. Have no ego, stop lying, shed your desires. Become like Uqab the first, like Gazelle the first, like Buraq, like Samir, like healer. Become weightless.

She looks at Gazelle and Uqab; she looks into the healer's eyes -- a flick of yellow swirls in a pool of light brown. Hearing the owl above hoot louder now, Dena flaps her wings furiously. With a final look towards the healer, she smiles, shouting thank you and goodbye. Soaring up to the sun, Dena spreads her wings as a ray of sunshine catches her, as if both owl and elephant were saying, "You will always be with me."

Two owls, one older, the other just weeks old, unite in the sky.

Wikifiqh

Mohd Faizal Musa

Mohd Faizal Musa, also known under the pen name Faisal Tehrani, is an award-winning Malaysian author and playwright whose works have been read across the globe.

We shall narrate to you one by one. We shall narrate it. So that you learn.

Grandma Zaynab said, 'In every book lies a secret, and each secret is in the Quran. It can be found in the opening letters of each surah.'

In the dark of night, Datuk Seri Prime Minister was visited by a gentleman who appeared very distinguished. He had on a creamy white robe with a black turban so dark it resembled a night without stars.round his neck was a cloth the shade of a banana leaf. The gentleman's beard was thick but tame. His eyes glistened like glass, making his face appear overcast. In his right hand, he held the Quran. The mysterious man appeared in Datuk Seri Prime Minister's dreams with the message, 'Gather all the knowledge in the holy Al-Quran for viewing.'

And so Datuk Seri Prime Minister gathered a crowd the learned: and with the help of philosophers, ulama, scholars, academics, and poets, he launched a project granted the name Wikifiqh.

At the press conference following the formation of the Wikifiqh Formulation Council, Datuk Seri Prime Minister stated, "We do not live for long. We must bequeath something for future generations."

The Wikifiqh project received global attention. So many ulama from the Muslim world came forward to contribute. The Muftis from Al-Azhar University and the University of Madinah also participated. Scholars from all four madhabs worked together. The funds received also spilleth over such that each member of the Wikifiqh Formulation Council was satisfied. Wikifiqh would be the answer to all questions. Ninety-nine days later, Wikifiqh was completed. All that was left was the launch.

Once more, the distinguished gentleman appeared in Datuk Seri Prime Minister's dream. This time, he wore a cloudy black robe with a turban the shade of coal.Wrapped around his neck was a cloth the colour of blood. His beard was thick and gnarled. His eyes, red, announced the sadness on his face that was covered in dust. In his right hand was the Quran. The mystery man proclaimed, 'There are still things incomplete. Pay attention to the letters Kaf, Ha, Ya, Ain, and Sad in the beginning of surah Maryam.'

Datuk Seri Prime Minister did not dare launch the Wikifiqh knowledge project as long as the true secret behind Kaf, Ha, Ya, Ain, and Sad remained unknown. But the Party Elections Director believed Datuk Seri Prime Minister must open the site to the public, to the people, to the entire world. According to the Elections Director, 'It is time the world knows the truth of Islam. Doesn't Datuk Seri Prime Minister want to assist The West in ending Islamophobia?'

Datuk Seri Prime Minister refused. However, the Party Elections Director was able to convince Datuk Seri Prime Minister that amidst the turmoil of inflation, the increasing cost of goods, the elimination of subsidies, and the collapse of morality, only Wikifiqh alone could guarantee Datuk Seri Prime Minister's victory in the elections and continued rule. The Wikifiqh Project would be the crown jewel of Datuk Seri Prime Minister's administration.

With that, Wikifiqh was launched. In the encyclopedia, the secret of Kaf, Ha, Ya, Ain, and Sad was explained as 'the muqatta'at letters.' They came in the form of hijaiyah letters such as alif, lam, mîm, sad, ra', kaf, ha', ya', ain, tha', sin, ha', qaf, and nûn,totalling half the number of hijaiyah letters. In the section of Wikifiqh on the beginning of surah Maryam it was explained that the muqaththa'ah letters are segments of verses that are considered mutashabih verses, meaning nobody knows their meaning. Muqatta'at letters appear in various forms and in many places in the Quran.

Why did the mystery man stress those five letters from surah Maryam? For instance, why not mention those from surah Sad, Qaf, and al-Qalam? Why not question the opening letters in the hawamim surahs, that begin with the letter ha' and man, such as surahs Ghafir, Fussilat, Ash-Shuraa, Al-Zukhruf, Ad-Dukhan, Al-Jathiyah, and Al-Ahqaf? Or even the muqatta'at letters in Al-Baqarah, Ali 'Imran, Al-'Ankabut, Ar-Rum, Luqman, and As-Sajdah. Or in the opening verse of surahs Al-A'raf Ar-Ra'd.

Datuk Seri Prime Minister found out that the five letters in surah Maryam appeared in a surah that offended the sensibilities of adherents of Christianity. Could Kaf, Ha, Ya, Ain, Sad be the formula to resolve the clash of civilization in The West, namely the Christian and Muslim worlds? Datuk Seri Prime Minister took an entire night poring over the paragraph in Wikifiqh on said surah Maryam. He discovered that all experts on exegesis surrender to the secret of the muqatta'at letters. For example, in the words of Binu Qutaibah, "not a single soul knows its explanation besides Allah." Binu Katsir attempted an interpretation, saying the letters were in fact the names of Allah. For example, alif lâm mîm means ana Allah a'lam (I Allah, am All-Knowing) and alif lâm mîm râ means ana Allah a'lam wa ara (I Allah am All-Knowing and Seeing). In the end, when the compiled writings of the tafsir experts were read, Datuk Seri Minister Prime found that Wikifiqh had summarised it as such: There is no one who understands Kaf, Ha, Ya, Ain, and Sad. Allah knows more about the meaning of the letters.

One night, the distinguished man appeared in the Prime

Minister's sleep. The gentleman still had on the black robe, black turban and red cloth wrapped around his neck. The gentleman asked, "Do you want me to reveal the secret behind Kaf, Ha, Ya, Ain, and Sad in the beginning of surah Maryam?"

His tongue numb, Datuk Seri Minister Prime could only nod.

The rich, thick-bearded man asked again, "As a muslim, what is your source of reference?"

Datuk Seri Minister Prime answered confidently, "Al-Quran and the sunnah of the Prophet pbuh."

The gentleman remained unrelenting, "After the Prophet pbuh is no more, who was able to interpret the Quran?"

Datuk Seri Prime Minister was silent. Then, he answered, albeit with some doubt, "The ulama. They are inheritors of the Prophet."

The gentleman shook his head. "They even failed at interpreting Kaf, Ha, Ya, Ain, and Sad. Have you ever read an authentic hadith about Imam Ali, as a doorway of knowledge? Let me tell you -- Binu Abbas narrated that the Prophet pbuh said 'I am the fortress of knowledge and Ali is its door. Those who seek to enter the fortress must pass through its door.' Now do you know what Saidina Ali said about those who attempt to interpret the Quran?"

Datuk Seri Prime Minister did not reply.

"Imam Ali said, al Mushaf bayna daftay al-kitab la yanthiq, wa innama yantihiqu bihi al-rijal. This means the Quran is mute, and is given a voice by interpreters."

"If that is the case, then was my answer just now correct?" Datuk Seri Prime Minister gathered the courage to argue.

"Your answer was wrong. The Quran is interpreted as however one pleases in your time. This is why the government you lead cannot triumph. You said just now, the source of knowledge for Muslims is the Quran and the hadith. When I asked who interpreted the Quran when the Prophet pbuh was no more, you could not answer. Know that the Quran is part of the Ahlul Bait. Abu Sa'id al-Khudri narrated that the Prophet, during his Farewell Haj, declared, 'Oh people, I am as if called (by Allah) and the time has come for me to answer this call. I leave to you two weighty matters (tsaqalain): The Book of Allah and my itrah, the Ahlul Bait. Verily Allah The All Knowing has told me that both of them will not part until the day they find me by the well. Pay attention to what you do to them after my departure.' Will you open the doors of your heart?"

Datuk Seri Prime Minister didn't blink an eye.

"Those with the right to interpret the Quran are the Ahlul Bait. They are the ones who know every secret of the Quran. They are the doors to knowledge. If you want to know the secret of Kaf, Ha, Ya, Ain, and Sad, then tomorrow morning go and ask the rubbish sweeper in your office. He is a man whose eyes have turned white from so much crying. His name is Yaakub." With that, the distinguished man left the dreams of Datuk Seri Prime Minister.

The next day, Datuk Seri Prime Minister cancelled all events scheduled by his assistant. He entered his office and said, "Find us a rubbish sweeper named Yaakub."

Not long after, the blind sweeper entered the office. Datuk Seri Prime Minister trembled. It was the man who appeared in his dreams all this while,except he was visually impaired, his clothes were tattered, and in his right hand was a broom.

"What is the secret of Kaf, Ha, Ya, Ain, and Sad?" Asked Datuk Seri Prime Minister, his knees shaking.

"It is the kernel of truth. Specifically, Allah bestowed them upon His prophet Zakaria from the Yaakub lineage. Prophet Zakaria a.s pleaded for Allah to teach him names that can erase his sadness for not possessing any progeny. So appeared Jibrail to teach him the names; Muhammad, Ali, Fatimah, Hasan, and Hussain. Each time Zakaria said the names Muhammad, Ali, Fatimah, and Hasan, he would always feel at peace, but the moment he said the name Hussain, his heart would feel tormented.Zakaria asked God, 'Why does my heart feel sorrow and tearful whenever the name Hussain is mentioned?' Then Allah said the muqat-ta'at letters Kaf, Ha, Ya, Ain, and Sad. Kaf is Karbala, Ha is Halakal 'ithrah, or the torment upon the holy family of the Prophet pbuh, Ya is Yazid, Ain is 'Athsyal Hussain, or the thirst of al-Hussain in Karbala, and Sad means Shabruhu, or the patience of al-Hussain. Upon learning the tragic tale that befell Imam Hussain in Karbala, Prophet Zakaria a.s cried and grieved.

"Prophet Zakaria prayed in remembrance of the ill fate that had plagued the descendents of Prophet Muhammad pbuh: 'Oh Allah, is it that the flower of Your most beloved and most kind-hearted Hussain, will experience such tragedy? Will this fate befall them? Will Ali and Fatimah mourn as I am now? Oh Allah, I plead, grant me a son who can cheer me up in my old age, and make him my heir and replace-ment. As soon as You grant me this child, put me through a fate as that was faced by your beloved Muhammad in relation to his grandson, Hussain.' Allah granted him a son, Prophet Yahya a.s. Oh woe, we now know the tragic end of

Yahya, who was slaughtered by Hirodus. The unblemished head of Yahya was paraded and flung to satisfy the heart of Herodia. Oh woe, how tragedy befell. Such was how Zakaria shouldered the pain of losing his son. And so he experienced the anguish Prophet Muhammad felt in facing the murder of Hussain in Karbala."

Tears streaming down his face, Datuk Seri Prime Minister sobbed incessantly at hearing the sweeper's story. Now he understood the relationship Kaf, Ha, Ya, Ain, and Sad have the substance of surah Maryam. Now there was a synergy between the severed letters, the muqatta'at letters Kaf, Ha, Ya, Ain, Sad, and the second verse of surah Maryam:

'(This is) to do with the abundance of blessings by your God (oh Muhammad), to His servant Zakaria.' And the verses that followed: (Remember the incident) when Prophet Zakaria prayed to his god with a prayer of supplication. He pleaded and said: Oh God! Verily my bones have become weak, and my hair has turned completely white; and I – my dear God – have never felt disappointed with my supplication to You. And verily I am worried about my brethren's carelessness in completing the religious duties once I am gone; and my wife is barren; therefore, grant me from Your side a son. A son who can inherit me, and inherit the family of Prophet Yaakub; and make him – dear God somebody who receives succour and is pleasing. (Prophet Zakaria was summoned upon the fulfilment of his prayer). 'Oh Zakaria! Verily We have conveyed news that will bring you joy by granting a son by the name Yahya, one We have never created before, not even another of the same name."

That instant, Datuk Seri Prime Minister understood the link Kaf, Ha, Ya, Ain, Sad have with verses 75 and 76 of surah Maryam as well, namely "Whoever is in error - let the Most Merciful extend for him an extension [in wealth and time] until, when they see that which they were promised—either punishment [in this world] or the Hour [of resurrection]— they will come to know who is worst in position and weaker in soldiers. And Allah increases those who were guided, in guidance, and the enduring good deeds are better to your Lord for reward and better for recourse."

Datuk Seri Prime Minister knew then that the kernel of the truth held secrets. Truth must be sought and unearthed with an open heart. Deviance would last for a time of unknown end, until there comes guidance in a sign from Him. So it goes, we have narrated to you one by one. Have you not witnessed it?

Love and Sorrow

Bethool Zehra Haider

Bethool Zehra Haider is a law student at UC Irvine. Her work has previously been published in Capsule Stories Magazine, Santa Clara OWL, and is forthcoming from the Berkeley Journal of Gender, Law, & Justice.

When I was a child, my grandfather taught me to swim. By the lake at the end of our road, a reflective pool surrounded by fountains of grass glowing in threads of gold, he pushed me gently into the water, teaching me the way he was taught—by survival. The first time, I sputtered and floundered about, vision blinking in and out, my lungs feeling as though they were being filled with a concrete-like panic until suddenly something clicked inside of me: when I stopped resisting, the water carried me up naturally to its surface. All I had to do then was stay afloat. After that initial pain passed, I spent my time in the lake in pleasure, staring at the sunlight from under ripples of water, watching it bounce about like warm honey. Our days grew long and languid, and my grandfather, though old, remained youthfully joyful. His past days as a school athlete were alive in the strength by which he carved the water in each stroke, pacing his breathing as waves divided around him. At the end of the day, we would wade out of the lake—usually me before him—and lie down on the grass by the shore, waiting for the sun to dry us off.

After the lazy sun had set and my siblings and I were prepared for bed, he would visit our room with his Arabic Qur'an, opening a page and narrating the tales like fantastical stories: colorful, imaginative accounts to rival any fiction we had read in school. Clearing his throat softly and sharing a shawl which smelled of sharp aftershave and mothballs, he would take us to worlds and times we never saw before. Yusuf, betrayed by his brothers, gripping me and my sister at the corner of our beds in anticipation, then Ismail and oh! Now a lamb for slaughter, all the way to Suleiman speaking to his hoopoe, filling our eyes with amazement to rival Sheba's.

As summer ended and the lake cooled, we prepared to go back home. My sister and I slowly packed our clothes,

preparing to greet our parents and reluctantly bidding
tearful farewells to grandfather. We saw him only twice
a year - during these summers and during the ten days
of Muharram. It was in this interval we saw him slowly
aging—eyes turning milky-white as his vision faded,
months where he stopped swimming laps of our lake and
instead paddled in a small circle, then only got his feet wet,
then left us to walk to the lake on our own.

Then one year, he didn't at all, and we spent the summer in
our home instead, wearing dark clothes for forty days, the
muffled sound of weeping from behind my parent's closed
doors. I was strewn apart and confused, my sixteen-year-
old feelings of grandeur cut short by his untimely passing.
We buried him in a patch of green grass which I could only
bring myself to visit once. Regardless of my shame at this
fact, seeing the earth that covered him cut far too deeply
within me to be able to relive the experience.

Five years passed and grandfather's house was left alone—
five summers, five Muharrams—until my parents decided
to do something about the place, and I, the eldest son, spent
my summer before college, a summer which coincided with
the month of Muharram, packing away as much of his life
as I could.

His house was as I remembered. I never before believed
people when they claimed the past is alive, but there,
around every corner, in my hopes, in the dog eared pages
of my grandfather's books, it lived. Walking into the tiled
entrance felt like wading into our summers, as if any
moment now his voice would greet me, his tea on the
counter would spill the scent of cardamom across the room,
his shoes at the door would give me a startled trip. Books
I neglected as a child, stacked up the walls, a dozen different teapots, the bed—dusty but still the same as when we

had left it, his desk covered in notes, drawings, pots of ink that smelled rancid but bled beautiful colors. One piece in particular caught my eye: a ring in which he had sketched out in Arabic, red ink bled upon a white page: inna lillah wa inna ilayhi rajioun. From Him we come and to Him we return.

I felt his eyes on me as I walked the hallways; everything had his name written on it, his fingerprints, his life abandoned such that I couldn't bear to put anything away. Instead I found myself unpacking things—going up into the attic to find his five allams and displaying them by the mantle, where he used to. The folds of the cloth unraveled in my hands as I unspooled acres of memory: images of my grandfather teaching me to point my finger when the salaam was recited, his eyes wet with tears at the very mention of the name Hussain.

My night, predictably, was spent haunted by dreams—little unalterable worlds, whispers of soul in which I found no solace or rest. And once they finished I was left with nothing but residual anxiety streaked upon my face; sad, desperate impressions, grasping a window of opportunity to enter this world. When I woke, sweaty and heart racing, I offered my prayers: two circuits of fajr to find calm.

On the seventh day, seventh of Muharram and seventh in his house alone, I finished my prayers and found myself longing for a familiar sound, a faint vibration of whispers trailing into my room—my grandfather, continuing his prayer. When I was a child and woke up alone and afraid of the dark, I would wait until I heard the floor creaking and listen for my grandfather's call to prayer as a source of comfort and assurance that someone else was out there. In days past, I would head downstairs to fill a glass of water for him once he finished. Today, with no whispering sounds of dua, I headed downstairs to fill myself a glass, hearing in the back of my head his gravelly voice saying, "paani piyo to yaad karho pyaas Imam ki." Remember the thirst of the Imam when you drink water.

Staring out the window, I collected fragments of my dream. A man standing and washing himself in blood. It was so bright—crimson against his skin, eyes ablaze, face and arms streaked with it, his eyes on me, filled with the flame of a madman. The memory burned through my stomach and I heard the echoed voice once again, "the primary ablution must be made in blood. The final ablution is always blood."

I swallowed, went back upstairs to sort through the boxes in his office, sun slowly peeking its pink light through the clouds, birds beginning to chirp, and ran my finger absently in circles along the circle of his sketched inna lillah. The primary ablution must be made in blood, I said to myself. There was no response. My grandfather's Qur'an was open on his desk. Next to it was a tiny red book, the words The Martyr written in gold inlay along its spine. Leafing gently through it, dozens of cards fell out—notes by my grandfather, written in red ink.

> *All of our prayer hinges on a single martyr.*
> *Without the martyr's blood, without the*
> *martyr's willingness to give life for the truth,*
> *we have nothing. We would all be lost.*
> *Remember that always. Without sacrifice,*
> *without majlis, without tears, we would have*
> *no religion.*

Seeing his writing woke something in me again, a frustration at seeing such evidence of his life and yet no presence. Why? A voice calls out within me. Why this pain? My movements now fraught with anger, I continued shifting things around as another notecard falls out:

> *3:169 – nay, they live.*
> *There is an ark of salvation / love once – climb*
> *aboard / love twice – bear the storm /*
> *love infinitely – and it becomes your home*

I thought of these words as day transforms into evening, evening into darkness. Nighttime is the keeper of secrets, the keeper of majlis, and I head to the tiny majlis in my grandfather's town, draped in black. Black is the deepest color: within it, magnitudes of depth and velvet mystery unfold into infinity, grief potent as the color. We lament the story of Abbas that night—moon of the tribe of Bani Hashem, his throat pierced with arrows, his niece's wish unfulfilled, a thirst quenched only with blood. Her pleas hung unheard under the moon. The same moon that rose that night, a miracle of following the lunar calendar: every year we stand in the same light, every year we dream under the same moon.

Night again, dreams again. This time they ran like shreds of silk between my fingers—if I grasped too hard in an effort to catch one it tore, so I had to open my grip and watch them slide through, powerless against the beauty and the flow.

A room, red from floor to ceiling. At the heart is a mirror, and in the mirror a light. I look up to see where the reflection comes from but nothing is there. The light burns brighter and I feel my pupils contract to hold the pain of luminescence at bay. I reach my arm out to touch it and it sears my finger, stronger and stronger every second, a burning intensity. But I don't move back. The discomfort, in some way, feels good, feels whole. I don't cry out, and as I reach the threshold of my pain, the red walls disappear.

I'm standing in my kitchen now, pouring water into my cup from a jug. I pour and I pour until water spills over the rim of the glass and I keep pouring, watching it on the table, down on the floor. The water keeps flowing. The jug in my hand refuses to empty, growing heavier and heavier, the water now a dedicated stream. Arm unable to hold the jug, my two hands begin to burn in resistance and the slow empty gurgle of flowing water heightens into a loud current. The jug falls to the floor, shattering into shards of glass, each individual chip spewing water in all directions, a pool of glass and liquid threatening to drown me. Feet wet, the water climbs up my legs, waist, shoulders. I want to yell, shout for help—someone, anyone, but my breath tightens in my chest and I realize I'm powerless to stop it, powerless to hold off. The air around me constricts and I feel an over-whelming sensation of nausea as everything turns pale.

I wake up suddenly, patting my legs, arms, face to make sure they're not somehow wet-- I'm absolutely dry—and head to the sink to wash before prayer. This time I turn the faucet on to the tiniest trickle and watch it drip out, slowly, slowly, each drop heading down into the drain, flowing so easily. I look up to the mirror in front of me and am unable to see my face. I turn to the other mirror and see it just as empty as the first. "Be," I think. My fingers reach out to touch its surface and echoes of my reflection suddenly bounce between the two surfaces. Multitudes of myself bounding through multitudes of mirrors. I turn back and perform my wudhu, watching how the face in the mirror drips with water where I do.

My anguish over my grandfather's death, the feeling of being alone in his house after so many years threatens to overwhelm me. I need a cup to pour this grief in, I think. An ark to salvage me. I'm seeing things. My grief is too big for me to manage alone.

I head to his room and spread open his prayer mat, green threads worn thin where his knees and hands would touch during prostration, his turbah dark from deep bows in the audience of God. I prostrate my head on his turbah to take a few moments to clear my mind, bathing in the silence, smelling the faint incense he would light while praying, still clinging to the cloth, the turbah he got from Karbala cool against my forehead, earth of purification, of healing, khaak-e-shifa.

Finishing my prayers, I remember a conversation we had once, sitting in this very room. Grandfather folding his hands together, long fingers knobby and callused, skin loose around his knuckles. "Do you know how all of this began?" he asks, a twinkle in his eyes and gesturing around us. I shake my head. "It was sorrow that began all of this. The sorrow of God. God, illustrious, all knowing, but alone. Unknown, except by his angels. God, A hidden treasure who loved to be known, absolutely unknown! Can you imagine that?" I shook my head again.

"What sorrow He had. Divine sorrow, from divine, absolute loneliness. And how did He cure it? By creating this world. Out of His sorrow, out of separation from His love, He made an entire cosmos! And suddenly He became loved by all. Worshipped by all. Known by all. Now not a person on earth is without Allah. Not an object, not a speck of dust, not a leaf slowly falling to the ground. None of it except with Allah's permission. And so sorrow became beauty. Infinite sadness became infinite glory. Eternal loneliness transformed into eternal worship. Infinite recognition. This is why our religion is nothing but love. We exist to love Him. We exist for Him alone. Sorrow is the push, love is the bridge, and His beauty is the destination.

"Sorrow gives way to love. And the sorrow leftover after He

finished creating the world was poured into a cup. The cup of sorrows, presented to all of us in the world before this one."

"Aalam e dharr?" I asked, remembering this from the Qur'an. After creation, every soul was brought into a different world, a prior world, and asked whether it wanted a chance at life. Those who said yes continued into the cycle of birth, our lives a product of our promises.

He nodded gently. "Aalam e dharr. But before we moved on with our lives, we each took a sip from the cup of sorrows, taking the smallest we could, trying to avoid suffering. Each one of us was eager to live but unwilling to suffer. And the last one in line, the one to drink the remains of all the sorrow we left behind, the one who bore all that Allah offered, who drank the remainder of the cup of sorrow—he was who we know as Hussain. We knew him then, admired him then, and we know him now and admire him now."

He paused to look at me. "Everything in life is because of those moments. Imam Hussain's sorrow is an eternal one. When the sky cried blood on Ashura it was because it recognized his sorrow—that same grief from whence it came. Our grief and our tears are not our own but a product of that grief from which we originated. There is nothing more natural, nothing more real for us to do, than to mourn the same sorrow we drank, the same sorrow we all share.

"We were born to mourn Hussain," he said, gravity unmistakable in his voice. What is so uniting about sorrow? I wonder. What is beautiful about death? Perhaps, while grandfather was alive it was a beautiful thing, to see his devotion and hear and hear is prayers. But now there's only emptiness where he once was. My grief boils out of me in tears and desperation, as I clench my fists. How is it fair? I wonder. How is it fair for us to suffer such grief? How is it fair for us, small humans living our small lives, to be forced to swallow immeasurable losses--our loved ones, our memories, all buried to be no more? How could we be made for grief? Made to tolerate such pain?

I spend the day neglecting any packing duties and instead wander out to our lake at the edge of the road. The water is glassy and still, and my face looks back at me. As I dive in, I watch my reflection splitting apart in a thousand ripples.

That night, we cry for many martyrs. I feel resistance in my body, some part of me trying to retain control, to keep my fears, questions, anger, sorrow in a bottle, to keep it swallowed and silenced. But tonight is the ninth of Muharram, and the weeping heightens at the mention of children—Aun, Muhammad, Qasim, Ali Asghar. Each one pure and unafraid, leaving mothers and fathers behind, leaving life behind and heading instead through heat and sand to battle trained warriors. Riding horses though their feet don't touch the stirrup, swords dragging on the floor behind them, three-day old thirst growing within them. The personification of absolute good fighting against absolute evil, they face no mercy or compassion.

Everyone weeps, the speaker unable to finish his sentences as he wracks with sobs. He wears a black turban upon his head, which he removes as he begins lamenting, an act of respect and despair, his head sinking into his hands. A symbol: nothing around us ever dies. The color black represents the life of the Prophet within him, his lineage traced directly back to the holy family. Perhaps the black is a boast, or perhaps the color is simply a matter of keeping tales alive, I don't know, but in removing the turban he directly salutes his forefathers. My emotions tighten in my throat with a feeling of white hot pain but I can't let them out.

The majlis passes in a blur, gravity from the next day weighing upon us, a sensation of something dreadful approaching, something painful growing beneath the curtain of everyday life. All night, men and women hit their chests in lamentation: poems read in tune, lines repeated by the audience, chants of "I am here, oh Hussain!" If the years had not formed such a barrier between us, I would have stood beside you.

We don't sleep, majlis continuing all night. I don't dream. The blood of Karbala is still fresh on the ground, the weeping and sighing of holy ladies, of mothers, of daughters, of sisters is loud enough to keep us awake. We cry, eternally, cry against injustice, cry against evil, cry against tyranny. We refuse silence.

Before the next day—that day, the tenth day—formally begins, I stand to call adhan, echoing an action taken 1400 years ago. I feel transcendent for a moment, as if this action is not a singular action I am performing and instead that it is eternal, a reflection of Ali Akbar reading the adhaan in the voice of his grandfather, calling his father, his uncle, his cousins, his brothers, his mother, his aunts, his family to prayer. The past does not die, I think. My voice is not mine today. My voice simply stands for a call that has sounded since then. When I finish, I see the faint shadow of my grandfather in my periphery, weeping softly while kissing his turbah, his bony frame shaking.

I begin to pray. I stand again, bow again, prostrate again, like I do every day. When we bow in prayer, we offer ourselves as martyrs; our spirits, our minds, our bodies, our necks open like Ismail's neck, like Ali Asghar's neck. And we rise, heading down to prostration as our foreheads hit the ground—that same ground where Hussain's forehead was laid in its last sujood, the same position in which Ali was struck his final blow. I feel something in me crumbling as a grief takes hold of me, an ancient grief. It's larger than my little concerns and questions, which disappear from my head. Every martyr holds within them a cycle of prayer. Every martyr, a reflection of God's light. All martyrs live in the names of their Lord, names that decorate our prayers and remembrance.

I turn my head suddenly, again certain my grandfather is seated next to me, sure I heard his weeping in my periphery. There's a sea of black-clad men next to me, bearded, draped in shawls as he was, but none are him.

 We don't greet each other. There is no happiness, no good morning, no peace. Lamentation runs day into night, the sun dipping down into its late-afternoon placement, turning everything golden-but-not-yet-pink, anticipating the sunset, anticipating blood, anticipating sorrow, and I feel my own tears on my cheeks. Prayer turns the hours into gold, weeping turns our day into that day, poetry turns the years back until we no longer stand where we are.

The veil of time feels thin. This is a day we live in the past, where the doors of mercy allow us into a fight where we weren't able to stand. The weeping faces of those around me, weeping, weeping as if we each lost someone so dear to us—didn't we?—weeping, as if the wounds are still fresh—they are, I see them—weeping as if the martyr's blood is our own. Is this insanity? Images that seem like a delirium passing before me. I can't sit up straight. My head is half-sunk in a pool of water, adrift amongst the sound of waves from another time, lapping lightly, tugging me away with them.

I keep myself hungry with a hunger that is not mine. I keep myself thirsty with a thirst from someone else's mouth. I hear my voice coming from dozens of people beside me, their voices coming from my throat. Our hands, in synchronicity, beating like hearts, beating upon our hearts.

The air gets hot, stale, weighted with the volume of our words. Poems live in the space around us, each verse a dense tangle suspended in the cracks, the little spaces in the valleys between the crowd—this army, thousands of years late, but standing still against a force whose face we see daily. One devil, who refused to bow to a command by God. One man, who stood firm against the slither of life the devil's insolence wrought. Speaking words whose proximity to truth opened his life to immortality. I hear rain pour outside—the sky echoing the fevered tempo of our rituals.

We walk back and forth seven times in Imam Hussain's footsteps. I, childless, young, am gripped by the pain of a father telling a mother their six-month old has been killed. Back and

Reality slips from me like the fabric of dreams. My grief over my grandfather bubbles over and blends with this larger, infinite well of grief over Karbala. Forth. Back and forth. The pain of a father, alone, unsure of how to explain his six-month year old's end. I feel my foot trip upon a turbah. Sand of Karbala. I pick it up, holding it in my fist as I complete my steps.

Back and forth,

I put the turbah again on the floor, seeing a spot where the sweat in my palm stained it darker. Is this what it was like, I wonder numbly. Sweat, heat, an impossible burden? I think dimly of even the archer who could not shoot because he kept seeing the face of a mother watching her baby.

Back and forth.

Time begins to grow holes. I peer through the windows it creates, close enough to feel the sting of dry heat in my nose. Day when veils fall and borders have no substantiation. I see into the past—past, what has passed? I am here. I am there. Am I alone? Each beat against my chest switches me between places. I watch them: absolute perfection undertaking absolute sacrifice. I know they watch me. I see my grandfather in past years, draped in black and crying into a handkerchief, his knotted hands tying the covers around the allams and striking his chest.

I step outside, cold rain over my burning forehead, the forehead of someone lost in a day long ago, the crazy head of someone intoxicated by incense and candles, spun dizzy by narrations and black cloth, red text upon black tapestry, the smoke from fourteen candles. I remember a story my grandfather once told me: each drop of rain is carried down individually by an angel, he said. An angel free to visit Karbala, an angel not tethered by space and place, an angel unbound by this frantic sensation I am caught up in—this longing, deeper than longing, this truth. Truth deep enough to sink in, to perish within.

Our sorrow is shared, I remember my grandfather saying. Our sorrow comes from the same cup. I feel the bit I drank awake in me today, tears coming from a place of divine insight, of divine empathy. Each mourner shares this loss. If remembrance keeps the dead alive, then what must mourning do? What must living their pain every year do? Alive in the eyes of God, alive in our memory, alive in our actions. The day, that day, this day, does not die. Women have removed their earrings; men wear the same clothes they have worn the past nights. Flags are carried, coffins borne from shoulder to shoulder, grasping hands desperate to kiss the effigy.

We inherit many things from history—language, land, appearance, habit. We inherit more than this, though. We carry the pain of our ancestors. We shed their tears. We inherit rituals that deepen upon us like wrinkles and crevices, like folds of life, like portions of our physical being. We inherit an infinite loneliness. Hal min nasir in yansurna?—is there anyone to help me? Is there anyone out there, any follower, any upright person, anyone opposed to evil who will stand, with their life, in its face? We inherit this lonely call because its question lives until now. And we answer it, here, today, in a day that is every day. We inherit the stoicism of a "no," a refusal to bow to tyranny, a rejection of conditions unacceptable, a rejection of falsehood. We inherit blood that is still red and flowing. We inherit one day from which we create our whole life. One day, the manifestation of all days, all struggles, all realities.

I dreaded packing away my grandfather's home like I dreaded the onslaught of Ashura. But the dread, I realize now, was a side effect of something greater. The size of my love is so big it caused me hesitation; I felt unable to wrap my arms around it. But once I give in, unfasten my grip, a soft lightheartedness eclipses me where I anticipated pain. Where I anticipated the emptiness of loss I feel held instead, a cushion fit for just my size. I fall comforted in familiarity: the smell of my grandfather's shawl, the incense in the mosque, the wick of candles burning. They carry me until I'm home again.

As the hours trail towards zero I feel a new grief within me, a sweet grief, at seeing this day go. We sit together again, gathering to say our final salaams. Seated in a darkness that grows into silence, our sadness becomes a thread tying us together; our hearts strung on the same cloth, worn out from the weight of mourning.

And in a final storm, my grief comes out in rivers, tears held back now pouring into the cup of Hussain, for my grandfather, for Hussain and a sensation of lightness overcomes me, the dense waters that were pushing me down before suddenly draining away. I look around myself at the other men, their tears pouring into the same cup as mine, together, replenishing what Hussain once drank and feel a buzz in my head, an airy wind through the chambers of my heart, the sensation of a first blossom, of pollen in the air after a long winter, of spring again. Where once the black walls looked weighted and mysterious, suddenly they appeared to be beckoning me into their folds, into something greater. A madness of sorts, a first view at the larger tapestry. From Him we come and to Him we return. The circularity of loss. What loss? I think back at myself. Arrival back to God releases the sorrow of separation, replacing back at myself. Arrival back to God releases the sorrow of separation, replacing it with the brightness of unity. My grandfather, gone now for five years but still alive in his home, in my memories, in what I'd carried from him. And vastly larger than him is Hussain, gone for 1400 years but still alive in his home—our hearts—in our memories, in the echoes of our actions and what we carry from him. There is a bubble of elation in my stomach, a faint, transparent bubble, but I feel it growing, growing, reflecting color and light and shine, the images of the world morphed in its spherical surface.

I wash for the final prayer of the day, a glimmering residue of water up my forearms, my face, a line on my feet. Looking into the mirror in front of me, I see only one face, worn by the day, shadows pressed under the contours of my eyes. But there's something else. A strange sparkle in the darkness of my eyes where there once was none. A strange excitement, pulling me towards my prayer mat, ready to stand again, bow again, prostrate again. I hear the call to prayer and rows of jama'at fall together.

Unsteadiness leaves my body and a coolness grows within me where there was once a fever. I feel carried among rows of people, and rise up in the communion. We lift ourselves from our final sujood knowing we carry purpose, surrounded by the scent of jasmine. We carry out that which he left for us. The change of day to night does not dim the feeling within me. I know this is something with life of its own.

As I prepare for bed, I watch the moon rise, a waxing gibbous just big enough for lovers to see the name of their beloved in its face. I think back one more time to that day, wonder if Lady Zaynab looked up to see her father's name in this same moon, at this same time. Wonder if she felt comfort seeing how the whole world was made to love her family, how the whole world couldn't help but display its praise for Ali, for his Lord.

I return alone to my grandfather's house, a new quiet surrounding me, watching my dreams from a distance. I sleep peacefully, knowing there is life to the calls from the past. I sleep peacefully, knowing all tears come straight from God's cup. And to Him they return.

This book was produced by
The Farthest Lote Tree Foundation

Visit us and view our other projects at *www.farthestlotetree.com*

www.ingramcontent.com/pod-product-compliance
Lightning Source LLC
Chambersburg PA
CBHW011153190726
48288CB00010B/3292